EVERY SECRET LEADS TO ANOTHER

SECRETS *of the* MANOR

Beth's Story, 1914

BY
ADELE WHITBY

Simon Spotlight

New York   London   Toronto   Sydney   New Delhi

Alfie
Vandermeer

Kate
Vandermeer

Katie
Vandermeer
Goodwin

William
Vandermeer

Eleanor
Wakefield
Vandermeer

Kathy
Vandermeer
Spencer

John
Vandermeer

Sally
Jameson
Vandermeer

Alfred
Vandermeer

Katherine
Chatswood
Vandermeer

Mary
Chatswood

The Chatswood

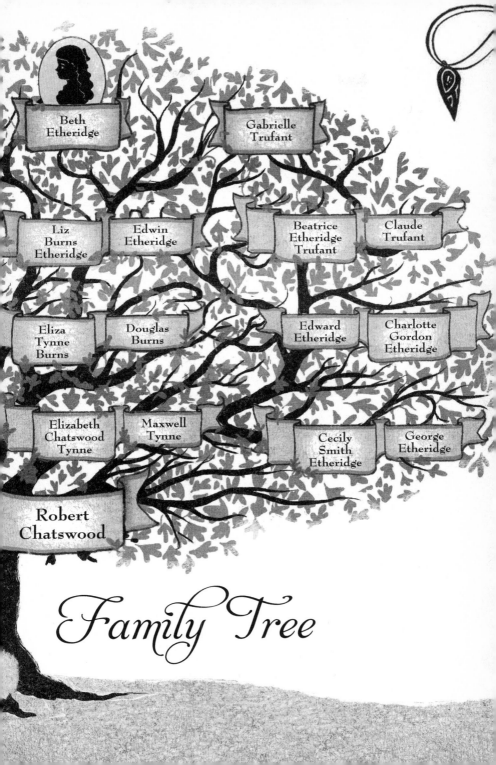

Beth Etheridge

Gabrielle Trufant

Liz Burns Etheridge

Edwin Etheridge

Beatrice Etheridge Trufant

Claude Trufant

Eliza Tynne Burns

Douglas Burns

Edward Etheridge

Charlotte Gordon Etheridge

Elizabeth Chatswood Tynne

Maxwell Tynne

Cecily Smith Etheridge

George Etheridge

Robert Chatswood

Family Tree

This book is a work of fiction. Any references to historical events, real people, or real places are used fictiously. Other names, characters, places, and events are products of the author's imagination, and any resemblance to actual events or places or persons, living or dead, is entirely coincidental.

SIMON SPOTLIGHT

An imprint of Simon & Schuster Children's Publishing Division
1230 Avenue of the Americas, New York, New York 10020
This Simon Spotlight edition June 2014
Copyright © 2014 by Simon & Schuster, Inc. Text by Ellie O'Ryan.
Illustrations by Jaime Zollars. All rights reserved, including the right of reproduction in whole or in part in any form. SIMON SPOTLIGHT and colophon are registered trademarks of Simon & Schuster, Inc. For information about special discounts for bulk purchases, please contact Simon & Schuster Special Sales at 1-866-506-1949 or business@simonandschuster.com.
Designed by Laura Roode. The text of this book was set in Adobe Caslon Pro.
Manufactured in the United States of America 0514 FFG
2 4 6 8 10 9 7 5 3 1
ISBN 978-1-4814-0632-1 (hc)
ISBN 978-1-4814-0631-4 (pbk)
ISBN 978-1-4814-0633-8 (eBook)
Library of Congress Control Number 2013943810

$\mathcal{B}$ridget, where *are* you?" I exclaimed. My hand hovered over the bellpull. I'd never had to ring for my lady's maid more than once. It seemed frightfully demanding to ring a *third* time, but I couldn't begin to get ready until Bridget appeared. And our chauffeur, James, had already left for the train station to pick up my French relatives, the Trufants. If Bridget didn't come to my aid soon, I would never be ready to receive them when they arrived!

I paced the length of my bedroom, brushing my auburn hair so that its waves tumbled softly around my shoulders. My hair, at least, I could fix by myself if I had to. But for everything else—from wriggling out of my billowing nightgown to fastening the tiny pearl buttons on my dress—I would need help. I glanced at the ticking clock on the mantel and realized that I had no choice but to summon Bridget yet again. If I wasn't dressed and waiting in the great hall when the Trufants entered Chatswood Manor, it would be a social catastrophe!

I yanked on the bellpull with all my might. Since it made no noise in my room, I had to trust that the bell to summon Bridget rang down in the servants' quarters. My hand had scarcely released the silken pull when I heard a soft knock. "Do come in!" I called without turning around. "Thank goodness you arrived," I continued as I began to rummage through a small drawer in my dressing table. "We have very little time, but if possible, I would love for you to weave the little pearls into my hair. Do you know where they might be?"

It was then that I looked up and saw, not Bridget, but Shannon, one of the housemaids who tended the upper floors, standing in my room. Her arms were brimming with peonies, lilacs, and the first June roses.

"Good morning, Lady Beth," Shannon said. "I've been filling the guest rooms with fresh flowers for the Trufants, and I thought you might like some for your room as well."

"Oh, Shannon, I'm in a terrible state!" I cried.

"What am I going to do? The Trufants will be here any moment!"

Shannon's green eyes grew as wide as saucers. "But, milady! You're not ready to receive! Where is Bridget?"

"Please, Shannon, you've got to help me," I begged. "I've rung the bell *three* times, and Bridget has yet to arrive."

"I'll go downstairs and fetch her myself," Shannon promised. Then she rushed out of the room.

I breathed a sigh of relief and tried to calm my nerves. Surely Shannon would not fail me. Ever since she'd come to Chatswood Manor two years ago, Shannon had been my favorite housemaid. The other housemaids tended to their work with little more than a hurried curtsy if I was in the room. Shannon, though, always had a smile or a kind word for me. She was so friendly that she never minded when I chatted with her while she cleaned. I knew that I could count on her to help me now.

I tried to pass the time by searching for my pearls, but the truth was, I had little idea of where Bridget stored such things. As the clock ticked away with no sign of Bridget *or* Shannon, I started to worry again.

3

What could possibly be keeping them? I wondered. Should I follow Shannon to find out for myself? Of course, I could never go downstairs to the servants' quarters—such a thing would be unthinkable. But perhaps I could wait just outside the staircase, or even ask another housemaid to help me find Bridget.

I paused before the portrait of my great-grandmother Elizabeth. "What would *you* do, Great-Grandmother?" I whispered.

From the canvas, Great-Grandmother Elizabeth smiled as she always did, with her lips closed and her eyes full of secrets. The Elizabeth necklace, a stunning piece of jewelry set with sapphires as blue as the sea, sparkled around her neck. Just looking at it made my heart flutter. Ever since Great-Grandmother Elizabeth had worn it, the Elizabeth necklace had been passed down to each Elizabeth in the family on her twelfth birthday. And it would be my turn to receive it on *my* birthday—in only two days' time! For as long as I could remember, I had dreamed about my twelfth birthday. There were so many exciting festivities planned: a picnic with my mother and grandmother, a formal family dinner, and my debut as the guest of honor at the grandest ball my parents had ever thrown. But receiving the Elizabeth necklace, the very same one that had been captured in the portrait, would be the most special of them all.

My great-grandmother's portrait had been painted when she was eighteen years old, just six months before she married . . . and six months before her twin sister, Katherine, left Chatswood Manor forever, taking with her the ruby-studded Katherine necklace. As the older twin (by all of five minutes), Elizabeth would've known for years that she would marry Cousin Maxwell Tynne in order to keep Chatswood Manor in the family. Her destiny had been set from the moment of her birth. But could anyone have guessed that Katherine's heart would lead her across the ocean to America, never to return? I longed to ask my great-grandmother how she had managed without her beloved sister by her side. I longed to see if my hair really was as wavy as Elizabeth's had been. And I wished to learn all the secrets that danced in her beautiful blue eyes.

But that was not meant to be. Great-Grandmother Elizabeth had died two years before I was born, so I had never even met her. Having her portrait in my room was a small consolation; I loved going to sleep each night feeling as if she was watching over me. Initially, Mother had objected to moving the portrait into my room, saying it was hardly proper decoration for a young girl's room. But I had begged and begged until she relented.

Katherine was still alive in the far-off state of Rhode Island in America, where she lived with her daughter, granddaughter, and great-granddaughter, my cousin. Lucky Cousin Kate, to live with her great-grandmother! I'd never met Kate either, but we wrote long letters to each other every week. That's how I knew that my American cousin had an adventurous spirit. What, I wondered, would courageous Cousin Kate do in a situation like this? Surely she would take action, and not stay caged in her room like a pet songbird.

I pressed my fingers to my lips to blow a kiss to Great-Grandmother Elizabeth, as I always did when I passed her portrait. Then, with my decision made, I strode from my bedroom. Mother was surely in the middle of getting dressed, and I was almost certain that Father was in his study, so I wasn't worried about being seen on my way to the servants' staircase. And, of course, there was no *real* harm in waiting outside it. It was, after all, just a few steps outside my room!

I hovered at the top step, straining my ears for any sign that Bridget was on her way. The sounds from downstairs were muffled, but I could faintly hear the hum of voices. Perhaps Mrs. Morris, the housekeeper? Or Mrs. Beaudin, our French chef? Then I noticed another pair of voices, approaching from behind me.

"Not a moment's peace until after the birthday—"

"Ha! There won't be any peace until the Trufants leave. I remember when Lady Beatrice—"

It was Jennie and May, who must have just finished sweeping last night's ashes from the fireplaces. Their conversation ended as soon as they saw me, and I of course pretended I hadn't heard a thing. With a quick curtsy and a murmured, "Milady," they descended the stairs. I watched them go, wishing that I could've heard just a bit more. *What* did Jennie remember about my aunt Beatrice?

At last, I heard footsteps coming up the stairs. I moved closer to the stairwell to see if it was Bridget, but it was Mr. Harrison, the butler, who crossed the threshold. And he was not alone; Mrs. Morris, the housekeeper, followed behind him. Then came Shannon and a gaggle of housemaids—Jennie, May, Nora, Peggy. But where, *where*, was Bridget? From the troubled look on Shannon's face—and the crowd of servants behind her—I could tell that something must have happened.

"Where is—"

"Lady Beth—"

Mr. Harrison and I spoke at the same time, but of course he let me finish first.

"Where is Bridget?" I asked, wasting no time on pleasantries. "Is she unwell?"

Mr. Harrison cleared his throat and looked purposefully down the hall. "Lady Beth, I regret to inform you that Bridget has resigned her position at Chatswood Manor, effective immediately."

My mouth fell open in shock. *"Immediately?"* I exclaimed. "Surely she didn't just *leave*—"

"I am afraid she is already gone."

Mrs. Morris stepped forward with a reassuring smile. "Not to worry, milady," she said. "Finding Bridget's replacement will be my top priority. And until then, I will personally assign one of the housemaids to assist you."

A hopeful murmur passed between the housemaids as my eyes met Shannon's. There was no mistaking the longing on her face. Suddenly I realized that this unfortunate turn of events could have a happy ending.

"Might I suggest that Shannon take Bridget's place?" I said.

Mrs. Morris paused. "Lady Beth, I fear that Shannon may not be prepared for the role of a lady's maid," she said, choosing her words carefully. "She has served as a housemaid for just two years."

"I don't mind," I replied.

"What about Jennie?" Mrs. Morris suggested. "She *is* the head housemaid. And she has a bit of experience as a lady's maid, you know. She stood in for Miss Dalton for two weeks last winter, and your mother was very pleased with Jennie's service."

"I would be quite happy with Shannon's assistance," I insisted. "We already know that she is ever so skilled at styling hair. Why, just look at those dainty curls!"

Shannon's hands fluttered up to the fiery red tendrils peeking out from under her white cap. "This is just a bit of vanity," she murmured as she looked down.

Mrs. Morris and Mr. Harrison exchanged a glance.

Since Shannon was still staring at the floor, I made sure to look directly at them. "Really, I can think of no better candidate for the job," I said firmly.

"Very well, then. It's settled," Mr. Harrison finally decided. "She can fill the role on a trial basis. Shannon, your work has always been impeccable, and I expect it will continue to be so."

"Of course it will," I said, answering for Shannon, who looked as if she might start crying at any moment. I knew they would be tears of happiness though, and that made my heart swell with joy. As far as I knew, there had never been a lady's maid at Chatswood as young as Shannon. She was just sixteen, only four years older than me.

I was about to grab Shannon's hands in my excitement when Jennie murmured, "Right, then," in the most disappointed voice I'd ever heard. Then she and the other housemaids slunk back downstairs—giving me a chance to stay composed in front of Mr. Harrison and Mrs. Morris. After all, Shannon and I could celebrate her promotion when we returned to my room.

I turned back to Mrs. Morris. "About Bridget," I began. "Why did she leave? And where has she gone?"

"Milady, you must not trouble yourself with such matters," she replied.

"But I can't believe that she wouldn't even say good-bye!"

Mr. Harrison gave me a pointed look. "Lady Beth, please excuse me. But might I remind you of the time? I expect the Trufants will arrive shortly."

The Trufants! I had nearly forgotten!

I reached past Mr. Harrison and grabbed hold of Shannon's wrist. "Hurry, Shannon!" I cried as I pulled her down the hall. "There's not a moment to lose!"

Shannon and I ran back to my bedroom as fast as we could. After she closed the door, I squealed with excitement. "If I didn't know better, I'd think *today* was my birthday!" I cried. "Can you believe it, Shannon? You're a lady's maid now—you're *my* lady's maid! Now we can chat whenever we want to and go everywhere together and—oh, Shannon, we're going to have such fun!"

Shannon's hands flew to her face. "Lady Beth, how can I ever thank you?" she exclaimed. "What you've done for me today—truly, this is such an honor—"

"Nonsense!" I said, laughing. "I'm ever so grateful to you for helping me. Oh, *goodness*, look at the time! Shannon, would you fetch my underclothes—they're in the top drawer, I believe—"

Before I had a chance to remove my dressing gown,

Shannon was by my side with a fresh chemise. She stood beside me, unsure, until I gestured to the back of my dressing gown.

"If you wouldn't mind . . ."

"Certainly, Lady Beth," she replied.

As Shannon fumbled with the small buttons that ran the length of the back of my dressing gown, I could feel her hands trembling. I turned around to look at her and realized that Shannon had grown pale. "Shannon! Do you feel faint?" I asked. "Whatever is the matter?"

"Lady Beth, I do apologize," she said miserably. "I'm just—I'm rather nervous. I don't know quite what I'm supposed to do. Mrs. Morris was right. I'm not experienced enough for a position with this much responsibility."

"She certainly was not," I told her. "You'll have the hang of it in no time. Once the dressing gown is unbuttoned, I'll put on the chemise. Then you can help me into the lace slip and then my dress. Then you'll arrange my hair and help me with my jewelry and shoes. And I've already brushed my hair today, so I'll just need your help with fixing it into a nice style. That's all there is to it, really."

"Are you sure?"

"Of course! And if you have any questions, just ask. You'll be brilliant, I'm sure. And, Shannon? I'd like to wear this nightgown tomorrow night so that I'll wake up wearing it on my birthday. It's my very favorite."

"Of course, milady. I'll wash—"

Shannon suddenly stopped speaking.

"What is it?" I asked curiously, twisting around to look at her.

"I just realized that I no longer have to do the laundry!" she said as an enormous smile spread across her face. "It's by far the worst task of a housemaid—the basement is so very dark and damp, and one hears such terrible sounds—"

"Like what?"

"Oh, a *scritch-scratch-scratching*, like a rat nesting in the corner, and Peggy said she once saw a *ghost*—"

"A ghost!"

"Well, I try not to pay any mind to Peggy, for everyone knows she lets her imagination get the best of her. But Peggy's tales don't matter to me anymore, because a lady's maid needn't trouble herself with such chores. I'll never have to go down to the basement again!"

"How splendid!"

"Of course, I'll see to it that one of the housemaids launders your nightgown at once," Shannon said, growing serious. "I apologize, Lady Beth. I didn't mean to complain about any of the work I've done here at Chatswood Manor."

"Don't be a goose, Shannon. I don't care if you complain," I replied. "You must always speak freely with me. I insist upon it."

Shannon's smile returned. "You are kind, Lady Beth. But I'm afraid that you'll soon tire of my chatter."

"Never," I declared as I pulled on my chemise. "Why, no one in this house ever tells me anything. So I shall rely on you to do so. Now, do you know what has happened to Bridget? I can't imagine that she would disappear so suddenly without a very good reason. Was there a scandal, Shannon? Did she fall in love with a boy from the village and run off in the night to be married?"

"I'm afraid, milady, that it is nothing so romantic as that," she said somberly. "Word came in the morning post that her mother has taken ill. Bridget left at once so that James might take her with him to the train station."

"Oh, poor Bridget!" I cried. "How dreadful! I do hope her mother will be all right."

Shannon nodded in agreement as she helped me into my lace slip.

"And which dress would you like?" she said.

"The violet one with the blue overskirt," I said after a moment's thought.

Shannon helped me step into my silk dress and then started fastening the pearl buttons in the back. I glanced at my reflection in the mirror.

"Which one do you prefer?" I asked Shannon as I held up two necklaces. "The pearls are perhaps more suitable, but the amethysts are my best jewelry."

Shannon seemed to consider both necklaces carefully before she replied. "I think the amethysts would look lovely with your gown," she said finally.

"Yes, but I had planned to wear pearls in my hair." I sighed. "Do you think the amethysts will clash terribly?"

"No . . . ," Shannon said slowly. "But if you want, milady, I could weave lilacs into your hair instead of pearls. They wouldn't conflict with the amethysts."

"Lilacs in my hair! What a charming idea!" I exclaimed. "Let's do that, Shannon. I should've known that you'd think of a clever solution. You've got a real knack for being a lady's maid, as I knew you would!"

Shannon blushed happily at the compliment and strung the amethysts around my neck. Then she checked the clasp twice to make sure it was closed. "Aren't you a beauty!" she said approvingly.

I touched the amethysts gently so that they would catch the light. I wondered if this would be the last time I'd wear them. Once the Elizabeth necklace belonged to me, I couldn't imagine ever wanting to wear another necklace—at least, not until I gave it to my own daughter someday.

"I was not at Chatswood the last time the Trufants visited," Shannon said. "Are you close to your cousin?"

"Oh, yes," I said. "On her last visit, Cousin Gabby and I were the very best of friends. I'm so happy that she'll be here for my birthday party. I know you'll like her, Shannon—she's so pretty and stylish, and she knows all about the latest fashions. I wrote to her four times this spring to ask for advice about what kind of gown I should wear to my party. But I'm afraid she never responded. I think she must not have ever received my letters! We certainly have a lot to catch up on."

"I'm sure you and your cousin will pick up right where you left off," Shannon said as she swept back my hair and wove it into a thick plait. "That's how it's always been with my cousin Molly in County Clare. Though years pass between our visits, she's like a sister to me."

"Have you always longed for a sister, too?" I asked.

"Of course!" Shannon said. "But that was not to be my lot, I'm afraid. Instead I've got six brothers, all younger than me—and such a racket they make! I don't know how my ma can bear it!"

"I would've settled for a brother or two," I said with a sigh. "But that's why it's wonderful to have you as my lady's maid now, Shannon! We can spend so much time together; it will almost be as if we're sisters!"

"You're very kind to say that, milady," Shannon said softly. I caught her eye in the mirror, and we smiled at each other. Right then I knew that I had absolutely made the right decision. Shannon was going to be the perfect lady's maid!

As Shannon finished dressing my hair with sweet-scented sprigs of lilac, I glanced out the window just in time to see the motorcar crawling up the driveway.

"They're here! They're here!" I cried. I leaped up from the vanity table and rushed to the door.

"Lady Beth! Your shoes!" Shannon called after me.

"Oh! I almost forgot!"

I paused just long enough for Shannon to slip them onto my feet; then I ran through the corridor and down the grand stairway as fast as I dared. Everyone was already assembled, of course; Mother, Father, and Grandmother were standing side by side with welcoming smiles on their faces. And just behind them were the servants in a neat row: Mr. Harrison and Mrs. Morris, then Father's valet, Benson, and Mother's lady's maid, Miss Dalton, who had left a spot beside her for Shannon. Then stood the most senior footmen and housemaids. It was an honor for the staff to greet our visitors—an honor that they had to earn.

With just one glance, Mother told me that she was displeased by my lateness. I smiled apologetically, knowing that Mother would understand when I explained about Bridget's sudden disappearance.

I scurried into position beside Mother just as Mr. Harrison stepped forward to open the great double doors. "Welcome to Chatswood Manor,"

19

he said in his most solemn voice. My relatives had arrived!

The Trufants swept into the hall, trailed by their servants: a valet, three ladies' maids, and two footmen. First came my uncle Claude, looking very dapper with his gold-tipped cane and his tall hat.

"Claude, old chap, good to see you again," Father said as he shook Uncle Claude's hand. "How are things on the Continent?"

Uncle Claude frowned and shook his head. "Very grave, very grave. A dark cloud is forming."

My ears pricked up right away. *A dark cloud?* I wondered. *Is there going to be a summer storm? But why would Uncle Claude look so worried about a silly old storm?*

Uncle Claude was followed directly by my father's grandmother, my great-grandmother Cecily. She had moved to France when Aunt Beatrice married Uncle Claude, so I didn't know her very well. Great-Grandmother Cecily was eighty years old, though of course I would never mention her age. But I knew what that meant: She was old enough to know Elizabeth and Katherine. They had grown up together.

"Edwin, my boy," Cecily said, greeting my father. "My, how you've aged. It seems that just yesterday you were wearing short pants, with your hair all in curls!"

I tried not to giggle at that image of my father as a child. He was so very dignified now, as the lord of Chatswood Manor, that it was hard to imagine!

Next came Aunt Beatrice, my father's sister, who waddled behind Cecily with tiny, mincing steps, as if her shoes were too tight. While Uncle Claude bowed low and kissed Mother's hand, Aunt Beatrice presented her powdered cheek to Father for a kiss.

"My dear Edwin," Aunt Beatrice trilled like a canary. "How very lovely to be back at Chatswood. How very lovely to be home in England once more!"

While our parents greeted one another, I stole a peek at Cousin Gabby, who stood behind her mother. I longed to run up to her. But I remembered my manners and waited patiently for our parents to finish. Gabby was fifteen years of age now, and she looked ever so sophisticated in her sleek pink gown with its narrow skirt. Her golden ringlets were held back with jeweled butterfly clips.

"Cousin Gabby!" I said as I reached forward to

embrace her. To my surprise, Cousin Gabby's hug was short and cold. But her smile was as lovely as I remembered.

"*Ma petite cousine,* how special to see you again. I must tell you, though, that Gabby is a child's name. I prefer Gabrielle," she replied. Then her eyes widened. "Are you wearing *flowers* in your hair? Like a milkmaid? Oh, *non, non, non.* I have been away for far too long!"

As Cousin Gabby—or, rather, Cousin *Gabrielle*—burst out laughing, I tried to laugh with her. There was no reason for my feelings to be hurt . . . was there? Surely she was joking, as I knew she would never want to insult me. But when I heard a giggle from behind her, I realized that her lady's maid was enjoying a laugh at my expense.

"Helena would like to speak with her counterpart," Gabrielle continued. "She wants to ensure that everything will be to my satisfaction during my stay."

I tried to smile as I gestured to Shannon. "This is my lady's maid, Shannon. She will attend to your needs."

"This is the one what has done that to your hair?" Helena asked in broken English. "No, thank you.

I require an audience with the housekeeper, *s'il vous plait*, not a country girl dressed up as a maid!"

I felt a flash of indignation at the way Helena spoke to Shannon and looked to my cousin to see if she was going to address Helena's rudeness, but she remained silent. *She's probably too shocked for words*, I thought. I tried to exchange a sympathetic look with Shannon, but she refused to meet my eye. A red blush crept into her cheeks as she blinked back tears of embarrassment. As Helena laughed again, Gabrielle finally spoke up and said quite sharply, "Is there no better way for you to occupy yourself?"

Helena immediately strode up to Mrs. Morris. "You are the housekeeper, *non?*" she said. "I am the servant of Lady Gabrielle. I am to tell you what my lady requires. She prefer a room facing west so that she may sleep in the morning without disturbance from the sun. Before bed, you must prepare for her fresh strawberries and cream on a tray with three pink rosebuds in a vase. The flowers in her room are to be pink and white. She despise the color orange, so please remove it from her room."

As Helena spoke, I grew more and more

astonished—each request was more ridiculous than the one before! I would've thought it was all another joke, like the one about the flowers in my hair, but Gabrielle stood next to me staring straight ahead as if there were nothing unusual about her requirements.

"You must be exhausted from your journey," Mother said as she patted Great-Grandmother Cecily's arm. "Would you like to rest before we dine?"

"You've always been a kind heart," Cecily said in her creaky voice. "Your mother must be so proud. Where is Elizabeth?"

Mother and Aunt Beatrice exchanged a troubled glance.

"My mother is Eliza," Mother said gently. "Elizabeth passed away some years ago."

Cecily blinked like she didn't understand. "What did you say, Eliza?" she asked Mother.

"It's no use, Liz." Aunt Beatrice sighed. "I can never gauge if she's more deaf or more addled by age, but either way, you won't be able to talk much sense into her."

"Pence is what I gave that ungrateful girl to run to the shops for a handful of sweets, and I daresay she ate them all herself!" Great-Grandmother Cecily snapped.

Mother moved her hand ever so slightly to beckon Mrs. Morris.

"Mrs. Morris, would you please show our guests to their rooms," Mother said. "I am sure they would all appreciate an opportunity to rest and freshen themselves. Perhaps they would also like to have something to eat brought to them at their convenience."

Oh no! I thought. If the Trufants ate in their rooms, I wouldn't see Gabrielle again until dinner. We could hardly have a proper catch-up in the dining room while the adults carried on some Terribly Important and Frightfully Dull conversation. There was nothing I could do but watch in silence as the Trufants followed Mrs. Morris up the stairs while our footmen struggled under the weight of their heavy steamer trunks. The Trufants would be visiting us for only three weeks, and then they were off to America for two glorious months—including a stay with Cousin Kate in Rhode Island!

At the top of the stairs, Cousin Gabrielle glanced over her shoulder and smiled as she gave me a tiny wave. That's when I knew that she had not meant to hurt my feelings. I wished that there were a way for us to spend the day together. Cousin Gabrielle was right about one thing: She really had been away for far too long. Suddenly there was so much I wanted to tell her—and so much I wanted to ask. How could I ever wait until after dinner?

Then I had a brilliant idea!

"Shannon, I'd like to see you in my room, please," I said.

"Yes, milady," Shannon replied with her head still bowed.

As soon as we were behind closed doors, Shannon reached for the lilacs in my hair. "Lady Beth, I am so very sorry," she said. "I did not mean to make a mockery of your hair."

"What? Oh, gracious no, Shannon. Leave them!" I said, ducking away from her fingers. "I am sure Cousin Gabrielle was joking, and even if she wasn't, I don't care! I think they're sweet! And every time I turn my head, I can smell their perfume. No, Shannon, I was hoping you would deliver a message for me."

"Of course, Lady Beth."

"Please tell Helena that my cousin is welcome to

come to my room before dinner so that we might get ready together," I continued. "And should she wish to join me *now*, that is perfectly acceptable as well."

"Yes, milady," Shannon said.

Usually at this time of day, I would write to Kate, but I didn't want to begin a letter when I was sure that Gabrielle would be joining me shortly. After several minutes, Shannon returned—alone.

"Well?" I asked excitedly. "Is she coming?"

Shannon shrugged and looked unsure. "I . . . don't know," she replied. "Helena said she would convey the message. At least, I *think* that's what she said. She can be . . . a bit difficult to understand."

"Then Gabrielle will be here in no time," I declared. "Shannon, would you please bring us some biscuits and tea?"

"Certainly, milady."

Before she left, Shannon scooped up my blue nightgown for the laundry. I settled myself on the chair near the door so that I could properly greet my cousin as soon as she arrived.

But Cousin Gabrielle never came.

3

After breakfast the next morning, I made a point to sit beside Cousin Gabrielle in the parlor. It was almost impossible to believe that she had been at Chatswood for almost twenty-four hours and we still hadn't spent much time together. Dinner the night before had been more lavish than usual, but I'd had a terrible time catching Gabrielle's attention. It was quite strange, but she had seemed rather disinterested every time I tried to talk to her about the plans for my birthday party. I'd been so sure that glamorous Gabrielle would want to hear all about it—the menu, the music, the mountains of flowers for decorating the ballroom. And, of course, the stunning gown that had been made for me by the best dressmaker in London. But Gabrielle scarcely looked in my direction and hardly answered when I asked her direct questions.

Gabrielle must be tired from all the travel, I told myself. Surely a good night's sleep, followed by a cozy morning in the parlor with Mother, Aunt Beatrice, Grandmother, and Cecily, would restore her spirits. But I was wrong again; Gabrielle turned her back on me and focused exclusively on Mother's plans to redecorate the dining room. To me, it was the most boring conversation in the history of England—and I think Cecily must have agreed, because she dozed off on the divan.

I couldn't understand why Gabrielle would rather discuss silk drapes with Mother than sit next to me whispering secrets. It almost seemed as though she wanted nothing to do with me. *Be sensible*, I told myself. After all, I hadn't done anything to offend Gabrielle. Perhaps we just needed a few moments alone to pick up where we'd left off—just like Shannon and her cousin Molly.

"Gabrielle, would you like to take a walk in the rose garden with me?" I asked as soon as there was a lull in the conversation.

"A wonderful idea!" cried Aunt Beatrice. "Gabrielle, I know you will enjoy seeing the beautiful English roses. No bloom in the world can compare."

But in the instant before Aunt Beatrice spoke, I saw it: A look of annoyance flashed through Gabrielle's blue-gray eyes. "Certainly, *ma petite cousine*," she said. "I know that you are terribly fond of flowers. But perhaps we can leave them in the garden and out of your hair."

Our mothers laughed at Gabrielle's joke, waking Cecily.

To cover my embarrassment, I quickly said, "Don't be too certain, Gabrielle. Once you see our roses, you'll want to wear flowers too!"

Then Gabrielle and I rang for our maids so that they could fetch our parasols. Helena arrived at once, but Shannon did not appear.

Gabrielle looked at me sympathetically. "Poor Beth," she said. "It's such a trial to have an incompetent lady's maid. You must speak to your mother about a replacement. I wouldn't stand for it if I were you."

"Shannon isn't incompetent," I replied as I rang again. "She is simply new at the position—that's all."

"You make too many excuses for her," Gabrielle said. "If she is not here the instant you need her, what is the point of her employment? What on earth could be more important than your needs? And look—now she is wasting *my* time as well."

"I'll just fetch the parasol myself," I finally said, ignoring Gabrielle's expression of shock as I stepped into the corridor—and bumped directly into Shannon.

"So sorry, Lady Beth," she said breathlessly. "So very sorry."

I glanced curiously at Shannon's flushed face and the loose curls of hair that had escaped from her cap. "What have you been doing?" I asked.

"Nothing, milady. I was—I was far from the parlor when you rang," she tried to explain. "How may I serve you?"

"Would you please fetch my parasol—the one with the ivory handle?" I asked.

"Right away, Lady Beth."

As I watched Shannon hurry toward the stairs, I heard voices coming from the dining room, where Peggy and Nora were clearing the breakfast dishes. I crept closer and stood just beside the open door so that I could hear them better.

"Put on airs, did she?"

"Oh, the worst I've seen. Thinks she's so special now."

"She's no better than us, I daresay."

"Never you mind. Jennie took her down a peg. We'll see how fancy she feels after spending every waking moment in the basement!"

Who are they talking about? I wondered. Whoever she was, I felt sorry for her. After what Shannon had told me about the basement, it seemed awful for anyone to spend so much time down there.

Then Shannon hurried up to me. "Lady Beth, I've brought your parasol," she announced.

"Shhh!" I whispered, but it was too late. Peggy and Nora looked up and noticed me standing by the doorway. I saw them exchange a worried glance.

"Milady! Is there anything we can do for you?" Nora said at once.

"No, I'm quite all right," I replied. "Thank you for the parasol, Shannon."

I quickly returned to the parlor for Cousin Gabrielle and led her to the gardens. The sun was shining brightly on the rosebushes, making their petals look even more vibrant than usual. There wasn't a single cloud in the sky.

"What a perfectly beautiful day!" I exclaimed. "I

hope that the weather holds until tomorrow. Last year, it rained buckets on my birthday, and we had to cancel the birthday picnic."

"Indeed," Cousin Gabrielle said, sounding bored.

"How did you celebrate your birthday?" I asked. "Was there a picnic?"

"*Mais non,*" Gabrielle replied with a short laugh. "I am not inclined to wallow in the mud like a pig."

"Oh. Well, what about a party? I'm *so* excited about my birthday party this year! It's going to be so grown-up, Gabby—er, Gabrielle. My party won't be at teatime, for starters, and we won't play any games. It will be a ball, and I think Mother has invited half the country! Can you imagine me as the guest of honor at a *ball?* To be honest, I'm a bit nervous about it. But Mother and Grandmother have been coaching me for weeks and—"

Here Gabrielle interrupted me by sighing heavily, as if she could hardly stand to listen to my chatter.

"So, ah, did you have a birthday party?" I finished lamely.

"No," she said. "*Maman* took me to Paris, and I ordered six new dresses for our travels."

"I see," I replied. "Your gown *is* charming, Cousin. I adore the embroidered trim."

A thin beam of sunlight slipped through Gabrielle's lace parasol and glinted off a silver locket around her neck.

"How pretty!" I cried. "May I take a closer look at your locket?"

"Oh, this? It is nothing. You could have it, for all I care," Gabrielle said as she pulled the locket over her head and dropped it into my hand. It was shaped like an octagon, with an elaborate letter *T* engraved on the front.

"It's beautiful," I said as I returned it. "Have you had it long?"

"No. I received it last month, on my fifteenth birthday."

"You must have been so thrilled! I can hardly believe that I'll *finally* receive the Elizabeth necklace on my birthday tomorrow. I've been waiting ever so long to call it my own!"

Gabrielle laughed harshly. "My locket is nothing like the Elizabeth necklace! The Elizabeth necklace is *far* more valuable."

"Well, the Elizabeth necklace is very special," I said agreeably. "Every Elizabeth in the family has worn it. And now my turn is almost here."

"That's not what I meant," Gabrielle replied. "The Elizabeth necklace is covered in precious jewels. This locket is but a worthless trinket made of silver, without even a single gem!"

I was so stunned by Cousin Gabrielle's outburst that I did not know how to respond. "But—it is—your locket is very lovely!" I stammered. "The engraving is so delicate, and the silver gleams in the sunlight. And what about this—the *T* must be for *Trufant*. Is it a family heirloom?"

"Yes, it has been in the Trufant family for two hundred years," Gabrielle replied carelessly. "But that does not make it valuable. I am still hopeful that *Maman* will let me wear her jewels when we are in America. It would be the shame of my life to wear this hunk of metal to Kate's birthday celebration. The parties they throw in America are probably the most lavish in the entire world!"

I gasped before I could stop myself. "You'll be in attendance for Cousin Kate's birthday?"

"But of course!" Gabrielle replied. "I would not miss her party for anything. *Maman* says that the very best of American society will be there. *And* I shall see the Katherine necklace. I wonder which will be more beautiful—the Elizabeth necklace or the Katherine one. Rubies are far superior to sapphires, so I expect that the Katherine necklace will be more stunning."

I was hardly listening to what Gabrielle was saying about the value of the gems in the Elizabeth and Katherine necklaces. Instead I tried to quell the jealousy churning in my stomach. Of course, I had known that the Trufants would journey to America after their visit to Chatswood Manor. But I hadn't realized that they would attend Cousin Kate's twelfth birthday party. I would have given *anything* to be there.

"I am sure you will have a wonderful time," I managed to say. Then I scolded myself: *Beth, you must rise above your envy. It is very unbecoming.*

"You must see my dress for Kate's party. It is the most beautiful gown I have ever owned," Gabrielle bragged. "And when I am in America, I will have five more made for me by the best dressmaker in New York. I do not know *anyone* who has gowns from Paris, London, *and* New York!"

"Indeed," was all I could say. *Where was her excitement over getting to meet Kate? Or how wonderful it would be to meet Kate's great-grandmother Katherine, a dear friend of her own great-grandmother?* How much my cousin Gabrielle had changed in three short years. It made me so sad.

At least our tour of the garden was almost complete . . . because I didn't know how much longer I could bear Gabrielle's rudeness without saying something I would surely regret.

Before bed that night, I wrote a letter to Kate.

9 June 1914

My Dearest Cousin Kate,

Tonight, on the eve of my twelfth birthday, I write to you for the last time as an eleven-year-old! I am all aflutter with excitement for what tomorrow will bring:

the picnic, the dinner, and, of course, the presentation of the Elizabeth necklace. And the following night is my birthday party! I've hung my gown just so in the wardrobe so that I can see it from my bed. At night I imagine myself waltzing around the ballroom, wearing my beautiful gown, and I'm sure I fall asleep smiling. I wish, dear Cousin, that you could be at my party. That would make it perfect.

I haven't had many opportunities to spend time with Cousin Gabrielle since the Trufants arrived yesterday. This is probably for the best. I find Gabrielle to be greatly changed since our last visit, and not for the better. I don't wish to sully her good name, but I thought I should give you a bit of warning since Gabrielle will be visiting you in a few weeks as well. How lucky she is to meet you. And even luckier to celebrate your twelfth birthday with you! Mother and Father stand firm in their decision that I am still too young to travel all the way to America. They say that perhaps when I am fourteen they will reconsider. Fourteen! That is still two long years away! I wish that I could stow away in one of Gabrielle's enormous steamer trunks and surprise you. But I suppose that sort of childish thought is one that I should leave behind, now that I am about to turn twelve.

Mother just came in to say good night; she tells me that I must go to bed soon so that I will be well rested for all the birthday festivities that the next two days will bring. I will tell you all about them in my next letter, of course, and spare no detail. I will certainly be missing you throughout it all, and wishing *that you were here to celebrate with me.*

With great love and affection,

I remain,

Your Cousin Beth

I was waiting for the ink to dry when there was a knock on my door. It was Shannon, bringing my bedtime tray of drinking chocolate and biscuits. Even though the June days were pleasant, the nights still grew cold. A cup of drinking chocolate before bed was just the thing to ward off the chill.

"Would you like to get ready for bed now, Lady Beth?" she asked.

"Yes, thank you," I replied.

She busied herself about the room, laying out a fresh set of underclothes and my second-best nightgown. It was as white as pure snow, trimmed with red ribbons and velvet roses.

"Oh, Shannon, I want to wear my blue nightgown tonight," I reminded her as I started brushing my hair.

Shannon paused and looked at me in the mirror. "I am very sorry, Lady Beth, but your blue nightgown is unavailable tonight."

"What do you mean?" I asked. "Where is it?"

"I am afraid it is still in the laundry."

I couldn't hide my disappointment. "But I wanted to wake up wearing it on my birthday! I wanted all of my birthday outfits, from morning till night, to be blue! It was to be a tribute to my great-grandmother!"

"I know, Lady Beth. And I *am* very sorry," Shannon said in a trembling voice. "But there is an unfortunate stain on your nightgown that will require additional treatment."

Poor Shannon looked so miserable that I immediately regretted my outburst. "Never mind, Shannon," I said. "I have other nightgowns. But I *am* curious— what stain are you talking about? I don't remember that my nightgown was soiled, just worn."

"It has a red stain on the sleeve," Shannon explained. "Jam, perhaps? Or cordial?"

"A red stain?" I repeated. "How peculiar. I didn't have jam or cordial while wearing my nightgown."

"That is strange," Shannon replied with a frown. "It's a stubborn stain, too. Ordinarily I would use lemon juice on a stain like that, but I fear it would bleach your pretty blue nightgown. But don't you worry, Lady Beth. I'll get that stain out and make your nightgown good as new. I will do my best to have it ready for you to wear tomorrow night."

"But I thought you weren't responsible for the laundry anymore," I replied.

Shannon's eyes darted off to the side. "Yes, of course, that's right," she said quickly. "What I meant to say is that I will oversee Peggy's efforts to remove the stain."

"Oh, of course," I said.

Shannon reached for the hairbrush and finished brushing my hair. Then she helped me into my second-best nightgown without saying a word. In the mirror, I could see her lips drawn together in a worried frown. I wanted to make Shannon feel better, so I glanced at my reflection and said, "You know, I think this nightgown is just the thing to wear tonight. Aren't the little red roses sweet? I have a feeling that Great-Grandmother Elizabeth would approve."

Shannon smiled a little. "Yes, milady, I am sure she would."

And the longer I looked in the mirror, the more I believed it.

$\mathcal{I}$ woke up with a start the next morning: My birthday was here at last! I leaped out of bed and rang for Shannon.

"Would it be all right if I were to be the first person to wish you a happy birthday?" Shannon asked shyly when she entered a moment later.

"Why, of course!" I exclaimed, giving her an impulsive hug.

With Shannon's help, I rushed through my morning toilette, eager to go downstairs for my birthday breakfast. Despite how quickly I'd dressed, I was the last person to arrive. Though Uncle Claude and Father were in the middle of a heated discussion, they both rose at once when I entered.

"My dear girl!" Father exclaimed as he took my hands in his and kissed my cheek. "Happy birthday,

Beth, and many happy returns of the day!"

"Thank you, Father!"

"Bonne anniversaire, ma nièce," Uncle Claude said.
"You grow more beautiful every time I see you. I think
you must not accept the Elizabeth necklace today, for
you will outshine it. A lesser beauty would be better
served by such a jewel."

I smiled at Uncle Claude's teasing. I'm sure it was
no secret that I could hardly wait to call the Elizabeth
necklace my own.

"Gabrielle, you must still be asleep." Uncle Claude
laughed as he nudged his daughter. "Go, greet your
cousin on her birthday."

Gabrielle rose from the table at her leisure and
carelessly kissed the air near my face. "Happy birthday,
Cousin," she said, but she didn't sound very enthusiastic.

As soon as I was seated, Father and Uncle Claude's
conversation picked up where it had left off.

"I am telling you, Edwin, that war is coming
whether we are ready or not," Uncle Claude said firmly.
"German expansion knows no bounds, and the rest of
Europe is too unstable to manage such overreach. The
situation grows more grave by the day."

Father shook his head. There was just a hint of a smile on his face. "Claude, Claude, you are worrying for nothing," he replied calmly as he buttered a crumpet. "It's 1914! The modern age is here! And as progress marches on, mankind works together for our betterment—not our destruction."

"You are an ostrich, with your head stuck in the sand!" Uncle Claude shot back. "You will not acknowledge what is coming until the bullets start flying. The country life provides too much shelter from the harsh truths of the real world. All this frittering about, fox hunts and afternoon tea—"

I glanced across the table at Gabrielle, hoping to catch her eye. But she just yawned and took a sip of her tea. It was clear that she had heard this conversation before.

"I say, now," Father said, sounding annoyed. "You've forgotten your manners, old chap. There is always a way to avoid war if one *wants* to avoid it."

I sighed as Bertram, one of the footmen, placed a slice of melon on my plate. It seemed that Uncle Claude wanted to talk of nothing but war. War, war, war, at every meal. I had hoped we might discuss something else on my birthday, especially since this war of his seemed to exist only in his imagination. After all, Father was right: The world was at peace! I would have changed the subject if I could have, but I knew that it wasn't my place to speak up when the conversation did not involve me. *Children should be seen and not heard*, I had been taught. If only Mother were at the table with us, she would be able to deflect such talk—but of course she took breakfast in bed, like all married ladies.

Then Mr. Harrison stepped forward to pour my tea. I was a bit surprised by this, because such a menial task is usually left to the footmen.

"Happy birthday, Lady Beth," he said in a voice so low that only I could hear him. "I should hate to spoil the surprise, but it might interest you to know that your mother waits for you in the parlor."

"She does?" I asked.

Mr. Harrison nodded, his eyes twinkling. "Yes, she rose early this morning," he replied. "I believe I saw a velvet jewel box tucked under her arm."

I gasped before I could catch myself. So I wouldn't have to wait all day! Mother planned to present the Elizabeth necklace to me right after breakfast!

"Thank you, Mr. Harrison!" I said happily. For the rest of breakfast, I occupied myself with thoughts of the Elizabeth necklace and all the Elizabeths who had worn it before me: my mother, Lady Liz; my grandmother, Lady Eliza; and of course my great-grandmother, the original Elizabeth. Such pleasant thoughts made it easy to ignore Uncle Claude's talk of war.

Then, at last, Father put his napkin beside his plate and pushed his chair away from the table. "Well, I suppose we should all get on with the day," he said to no one in particular.

"I beg your pardon, Lord Etheridge," Mr. Harrison said, staring straight ahead. "Lady Liz has requested the pleasure of everyone's company in the parlor."

"Oh yes, of course," Father said. He turned to me and held out his arm. "Beth?"

I felt very grown-up on Father's arm as we walked to the parlor. Mother was standing by the Chinese lacquer cabinet, beneath the portrait of Elizabeth and Katherine that had been painted when they were twelve years old. It was a very special portrait of the twins, for they were wearing their necklaces, but a sad one too;

their mother, Lady Mary, had died just months before. Those precious necklaces, which had come to mean so much to so many generations, had been Lady Mary's last gift to her daughters.

"Dear Beth," Mother said, smiling warmly as she placed the jewel box atop the cabinet and extended her arms to me.

Father led me to the front of the room, where Mother and Grandmother embraced me.

"On this day, we mark the passing of twelve years since your birth," Mother began. "Today, my dearest girl, the door on your childhood begins to close. Your future unfurls before you, bringing with it all the responsibilities belonging to a lady of Chatswood Manor. The people will look to you, Beth, and you must remember the example you set for them in all that you say and do."

"Yes, Mother," I said as I nodded my head.

"And with these duties come many privileges," continued Mother. "Including this one, which you will wear around your neck: the Elizabeth necklace, given to every eldest daughter in our line since Lady Elizabeth Chatswood Tynne wore it first. It gives me great joy, my daughter, to present these precious jewels to you today."

Grandmother stepped next to Mother, and together they opened the lid of the jewel box and drew out the Elizabeth necklace. Mother cradled the pendant in her palm while Grandmother gently held the long chain to keep it from getting tangled.

"Turn around, my dear," Mother said.

I closed my eyes as Mother slipped the Elizabeth necklace around my neck. It was heavier than I had expected, and the gold felt warm, as if it had retained the heat from all of the Elizabeths before me who had worn it. And yet, from the moment the pendant touched my chest, it felt as if it had always been a part of me.

Mother gently turned me back to face her. Tears shone in her beautiful blue eyes. "Happy birthday, my darling," she whispered, kissing my face.

Behind her, Grandmother used a dainty lace handkerchief to wipe away a tear. "I still remember when my mother gave the necklace to me," she said. "I know that many people were shocked she would do such a thing. Everyone expected Lady Elizabeth to wear that necklace to her dying day. But she was firm in her conviction that there was no better way to mark a girl's twelfth birthday. Receiving the necklace from her was the proudest moment of my life."

"I remember how special it was when the two of you gave the Elizabeth necklace to me," Mother said to her. "It was during my birthday party, and everyone left the ballroom to watch, filling the parlor to capacity! I was so nervous with all those eyes on me; my knees were knocking so that I could barely walk. Grandmother Elizabeth smiled at me, as though she knew that all would be well. And she was right."

"I wish she could be here today," I said softly.

"So do I," Mother replied. "So do I."

Grandmother reached for our hands. "My dears, she is here," Grandmother said. "In spirit, she is with us, and she has never been more pleased."

"Wrong! That's wrong, all wrong!"

The three of us jolted as though an electric shock had passed through us. That harsh voice rang in my ears—*wrong, all wrong*—as Cecily tottered toward me. Her hand was like a claw as she grasped my lovely Elizabeth necklace. Cecily peered closely at it, and her entire face twisted into a disapproving frown.

"You've got the wrong necklace, my girl!" she announced.

Father was on his feet at once. "Now, Grandmother," he said to Cecily. "This is very unbecoming."

"I should say so!" Cecily snapped at him. "All this pomp and they've given the girl the Katherine necklace! You've made a laughingstock of tradition!"

My grandmother frowned. "I can assure you, *Cecily*, that we have given Beth the correct necklace."

"The *Katherine* necklace has blue stones. The *Elizabeth* necklace has red. So it has been, so it shall always be," Cecily said firmly. "I should know. I was close friends with the twins and saw them wearing their necklaces countless times."

I turned away from Cecily by instinct, my hands protectively covering the Elizabeth necklace. *Could it be?* I wondered. *Could this be the wrong necklace?*

Aunt Beatrice spoke up. "It was a great many years ago, Grandmother. I'm sure you're just confused."

"You're a fine one to talk about confusion," Cecily retorted. "I remember like it was yesterday. Lady Mary had had the necklaces specially made, you see—before her death. And she made sure that each girl would receive a necklace with her favorite color. Blue for Katherine, red for Elizabeth. They wore their necklaces to their birthday party the very evening they received them, and I was there! Katherine in the blue necklace and Elizabeth in the red."

Everything Cecily was saying sounded right—except, of course, the part about which necklace belonged to which girl. But other than that detail, it seemed that Cecily had remembered everything correctly.

Mother gave Aunt Beatrice a pointed look.

"Gabrielle," Aunt Beatrice said. "Your great-grandmother is tired. Please take her to her room."

"Just ring for Paulette," replied Gabrielle. "She can take her."

"You'll do it *now*," Aunt Beatrice said through gritted teeth.

With a heavy sigh, Gabrielle flounced off the divan. "Come, Great-Grandmother," she said.

"I tell you, the necklace is *wrong*!" Cecily grumbled as Gabrielle led her from the room.

Mother patted my hand in a reassuring way. "You mustn't give what Cecily said another thought, my darling," she said. "She is very old, and senility gets the better of her sometimes."

"Yes, Mother," I said. The truth was I wasn't a bit bothered by Cecily's outburst. To think that there could be a long-lost secret—*perhaps even a scandal!*—embedded in the Elizabeth necklace alongside its sapphires gave me a tremendous thrill. I desperately wanted to go straight to my room and write to Cousin Kate about it!

"Harrison, my good man," Father suddenly said. "Bring that box to me now, would you?" I wondered what box Father was referring to, but I didn't have to wonder for long. Moments later, Mr. Harrison returned with the box Father had requested. He handled it with great care.

"Excellent, Harrison, thank you!" Father exclaimed. "Look at it. Just look at it!"

I glanced inside the box at the strangest contraption I had ever seen. It had odd switches and knobs, and the middle section was folded like an accordion.

"Oh, Edwin." Mother sighed, shaking her head.

"It's the very latest—an Eastman Kodak!" he said proudly. Then, upon seeing my confusion, he continued,

"A camera, dear girl, for photography! I thought we should commemorate your birthday in the modern style!"

"*A photograph?*" Mother said in dismay. "Beth will sit for a portrait, just as all the other Elizabeths have upon receiving the necklace."

My grandmother, who looked as shocked as my mother, nodded in agreement.

"I see no reason why she can't do both," Father told them. "Come, let me take a photograph today—of the three Elizabeths: my wife, her mother, and my daughter, the birthday girl. Then I'll take the film to London for development."

"Quite an inconvenience, really," Mother replied. "Quite a headache. Taking film to London, waiting for it to be processed, receiving the prints by post . . ."

But Father was not to be discouraged. "You're quite right, my dear," he said smoothly. "You know, it might be wise to purchase one of those development machines. Or we could even build a darkroom here at Chatswood. Yes. I say, Harrison? Do any of the footmen fancy a turn as a developer? Someone we could trust to be mindful of the chemicals and such?"

"I would be happy to make inquiries, sir," Mr. Harrison replied.

"Today is not the time for this discussion," Mother said firmly. "It is Beth's birthday, and we have a great deal to do today and tomorrow. Now, Edwin, we will pose for *one* photograph, and then it will be time for us to get ready for the birthday picnic."

I stood beneath the portrait of Elizabeth and Katherine, flanked on either side by my mother and grandmother, while Father fiddled with the switches and lenses. As soon as the flash went *pop!*, Mother glanced at the clock on the mantelpiece. "Beth, run and change for the picnic," she told me.

"Yes, Mother," I replied, hurrying out of the room. What a fantastic morning this had been so far! I'd received the Elizabeth necklace, witnessed Cecily's proclamation about a family scandal, *and* posed for a modern photograph! I could hardly wait for the festivities to continue!

As I reached the corridor outside my room, I noticed Shannon and Helena having a conversation near my door. I slowed down a bit to see if I could hear what they were talking about.

"Is there something you need?" Shannon asked Helena.

"I am fine, thank you," Helena replied.

Shannon tried again. "What I'm trying to say is that anything required for Lady Gabrielle will be found directly outside her room," she said. "So if I can help in any way—"

"You can help by minding your business!" Helena snapped rudely.

"Lady Beth's laundry chute *is* my business!" said Shannon. "You will find Lady Gabrielle's laundry chute at the other end of the corridor. And so I'll kindly ask you again to tell me what you just put down Lady Beth's laundry chute so that I may retrieve it for you."

Helena suddenly went very pale. "What is this . . . *laund-a-ree choot?*" she asked, stumbling over the unusual words.

Shannon's brow furrowed. "Why, Helena, it's—"

At that moment, Helena spotted me. Her expression was a mix of anger and fear. She spun around and marched away from Shannon—but not before repeating, "Mind your business, housemaid!"

"What was *that* about?" I asked Shannon as I approached.

"Lady Beth," Shannon said. "Very sorry you had to witness that on your birthday."

"Helena seemed so angry," I continued as Shannon followed me into my bedroom.

Shannon shrugged. "She *is* an odd one, Lady Beth," she said in a confidential tone. "But to be honest, I think she struggles more with the language than she cares to admit. I was simply trying to explain where Helena would find Lady Gabrielle's laundry chute, though I don't think she understood me at all."

"I see," I said, turning my attention to the wardrobe.

An argument over the laundry was much less interesting than the row of blue gowns before me.

"Shannon, which dress do you think is best?" I asked. I was very glad that I could ask her advice. Not even Shannon's stiff uniform could hide how stylish she was—from her smart buckled boots to the fine lace at her collar. It was prettier than all the housemaids' collars; Shannon must have sewn it herself.

Shannon tapped her chin as she studied each gown. "Truly, they're all lovely," she said at last. "But if it were my choice, I'd wear the one with the pale blue stripes. I think it's just the thing for a picnic."

"Yes, you're absolutely right," I replied.

"Let me unfasten your necklace before you change," Shannon continued. "I'd hate for the sapphires to catch your silk gown."

With my hand to my throat, I felt the weight of the Elizabeth necklace as it dropped into my palm. It was still so hard to believe that it belonged to me! I realized that Shannon wouldn't have had the opportunity before now to see the necklace up close, so I held it out to her.

"Oh, may I?" she asked eagerly.

"Of course!"

Shannon held the necklace as if it were the most precious thing in all the world. "It's a marvel," she whispered. "The shine of the gold and the sparkle of the sapphires—oh, Lady Beth, what a treasure."

"You could try it on, if you want," I offered.

But Shannon shook her head vehemently. "No, never!" she replied. "The Elizabeth necklace belongs to you and only you, Lady Beth. It shouldn't grace another neck until you give it to your own daughter."

I smiled at Shannon in the mirror. A daughter of my own—the next Elizabeth—seemed like such a far-away thing that I could hardly imagine it.

"It's so special to have an heirloom like this," Shannon said as she held the gown open for me.

"Yes, I know," I replied. "When I walked with Gabrielle in the gardens, she was so disdainful of her own heirloom locket. And all because it was engraved instead of set with gems."

Shannon shook her head. "A pity," she said. "I can only hope that Lady Gabrielle will come to appreciate her heirloom as she grows."

Then a self-conscious smile flickered across

Shannon's face. "I have one," she said. "Would you care to see it?"

"Of course I would!" I cried.

Shannon reached into the high neck of her dress and pulled out a simple metal chain. A bronze medallion dangled from it.

"It's a Saint Anthony medal," Shannon explained. "He's the patron saint of lost things and missing people, you know. It belonged to my gram. When she was a girl, she had an awful knack for losing things. And when it was time for her to go into service, Gram was scared half to death that she'd lose something belonging to the lady of the house. Her mum gave her this medal so that Gram could call on Saint Anthony if she did.

"When I went into service, Gram gave it to me," Shannon continued. "I know it's not much to look at, and worth even less than you'd think, but it's the most special thing I own."

"I think it's beautiful," I said firmly—and I meant it.

Shannon bowed her head, but I could see how pleased she was. "That's very kind of you, milady," she said as she finished fastening the buttons on my gown.

"Now, shall we return the Elizabeth necklace to its rightful place?"

I watched in the mirror as Shannon fastened the clasp around my neck.

"You look as pretty as a summer morn," Shannon declared as she inspected my ensemble to make sure no detail had been overlooked.

"Thank you, Shannon. I would be lost without you!" I told her.

We joined Mother and Grandmother and their maids in the foyer. Then we all proceeded to the garden for my picnic. A crisp white tent had been erected near the roses; beneath it, a small table was elegantly laid with blue-edged china and Great-Grandmother Elizabeth's silver tea service. Bertram and Arnold stood to the side, ready to serve us from a large hamper that Mrs. Beaudin had filled to the brim.

"A beautiful day for a beautiful girl!" Grandmother exclaimed as we took our seats. "My, I can't remember when the weather smiled on us so prettily."

"That's as it should be," Mother replied, fixing me with a warm smile. "I want everything just so for Beth's twelfth birthday. Even the weather must cooperate!"

We all laughed at her little joke.

"Tell me a story," I said as Bertram placed two delicate sandwiches on my plate. "One about Elizabeth and Katherine."

"But my dear, we've already told you so many," Grandmother replied. "I daresay you know them all by heart."

I smiled sheepishly. "Even so, I love to hear them. And there's still so much I don't know! For example— what were Great-Grandmother Elizabeth's hobbies?"

"That I remember well," Grandmother said. "My mother loved poetry and writing. She could turn a pretty phrase, you know. Not that she'd ever boast of such a thing."

"Indeed, Grandmother Elizabeth was quite private about it," Mother recalled. "I remember going into her room when I was a small girl—she'd let me visit her while she dressed for dinner—and finding a locked drawer with a key jutting from it. I'm afraid my curiosity got the better of me, and I unlocked it. There was just one item inside: a thin leather book, secreted away so that no one but her could read it."

"What was in it?" I asked eagerly. No one had ever

told me that my great-grandmother loved writing as much as I did.

"Before I could read a word, Elizabeth was at my side. She gently took the key from my hand and locked the drawer. I never saw the book—or the key—again."

"But where are they now?"

Mother and Grandmother exchanged a glance. "You know, Beth, I can't say," Grandmother replied. "Liz, were her poems and papers shelved in the library after she passed?"

"I don't think so," Mother said, shaking her head. "I'm sure they're somewhere, though. I do remember this, Beth—she loved chocolate. Just like you! Arnold, please bring us the Florentine biscuits. As it's a special occasion, I see no reason why Beth should wait for them."

"Begging your pardon, milady," Arnold said, "but Mrs. Beaudin asked me to convey her deepest apologies that there are no Florentine biscuits today."

"And why not?" asked Mother sharply. "They were on the menu."

"There was . . . an unfortunate incident in the kitchen," Arnold replied. "If Lady Beth would like, there are three kinds of cake and strawberry ice instead."

"Strawberry ice!" I cried. "Yes, please!"

Mother smiled indulgently as she pushed aside my plate of sandwiches. "The perfect start to a picnic," she declared. "I'll have some too."

I had such a lovely time with my mother and grandmother that I hardly noticed that my favorite biscuits were missing. As we began the walk back to Chatswood Manor, I was so content that I thought, *I hope nothing will ever change the way things are right now.*

But we had scarcely returned when a terrifying scream pierced my ears!

6

A chill crawled over my body, despite the warmth of the day. "Oh, Mother, what was that?" I exclaimed, reaching for her arm.

"It came from inside the house," she said, her lips set in a tight, thin line. "Hurry, Beth."

The scream came again.

We ran up the steps and burst into the great hall, only to find Cousin Gabrielle atop the stairs, her mouth open as if she were about to scream. At that moment, Aunt Beatrice rushed up to her, followed by Father and Uncle Claude, who must've just returned from their tour of the grounds.

"Gabby, what is it? What's happened?" Aunt Beatrice cried. "Are you ill? Tell me, pet. Tell me!"

"Gone!" Gabrielle screamed. "It's gone. It's gone!"

"*What's* gone?"

"My Trufant locket!" Gabrielle shrieked. She appeared to wobble on her feet, and my heart clenched; if she fainted at the top of the stairs and fell, her injuries would be dreadful. I was not the only one who thought that, as Uncle Claude and my father immediately rushed to her side and helped carry Gabrielle down the stairs.

Aunt Beatrice began fanning Gabby with her lace fan. "Liz, we need smelling salts," she called over her shoulder.

"Of course," Mother said, nodding at Miss Dalton.

By this time, a large crowd had gathered in the hall: all the Trufants and all the Etheridges, and a great many servants as well. Gabrielle's eyelids fluttered dramatically, and I thought it looked like she was peeking at the crowd to see how much attention she had attracted. But I was probably mistaken.

After Miss Dalton returned with the smelling salts, Aunt Beatrice waved the vial delicately in front of Gabrielle's face. Gabrielle opened her eyes wide— and burst into tears.

"Oh, *Maman*, *Maman*, my Trufant locket has been *stolen*!" Gabrielle wailed. "My most precious Trufant locket, stolen!"

Uncle Claude's shoulders stiffened. "I demand that the house be searched at once," he announced, "starting with the staff quarters."

"Surely Gabrielle's locket has just been misplaced," Father began.

"Stolen!" Gabrielle interjected. "Stolen from my room!"

"Do you refuse me?" Uncle Claude snapped. "Really, Edwin, that such a thing should happen in *your* house—"

Father raised his hands to calm Uncle Claude. "Now, now," he said. "Of course we will search the house. I have full faith in our staff, Claude. They are good people, hardworking and honest. Chatswood Manor does not employ thieves! I am confident that the locket will turn up in due time, and I'm sure we'll all have a good laugh about it. Harrison!"

"Yes, sir," Mr. Harrison said as he stepped forward.

"Organize a search party, would you? Make sure that no stone goes unturned, as they say," Father told him.

Mr. Harrison nodded briskly. "Mrs. Morris and I will search the staff quarters ourselves," he said.

"Oh, it's *gone!*" Gabrielle cried again. Her shoulders shook with sobs. But as she covered her face with her hands, it seemed to me that she was not really weeping, but merely pretending to. "What shall I do without it?"

Aunt Beatrice threw her arms around Gabrielle. "There, there," she crooned. "You mustn't cry so. If your locket doesn't turn up, Papa will buy you a new one, won't you, Claude?"

"Yes, of course," Uncle Claude answered.

Gabrielle's sobs quieted at once. "One made of gold? *Real* gold?" she asked. "And set with precious gems of my choosing?"

"Anything you desire, *ma princesse*," Uncle Claude declared.

An uneasy feeling settled over me. I couldn't forget the disdain that Gabrielle had expressed for the Trufant locket on our walk yesterday. How convenient that it should suddenly disappear, inspiring her parents to promise her a brand-new—and much fancier—replacement. I knew that this opinion was terribly uncharitable. *You should give your cousin the benefit of the doubt*, I told myself. Yet I couldn't shake the feeling that Gabrielle was somehow being dishonest.

At that moment, Gabrielle's eyes met mine. She might have guessed my thoughts, because she immediately flung herself into her mother's arms, crying out, "Gone! Gone forever! Oh!"

I decided then that I had little patience left for my cousin—especially since I knew her true feelings for the Trufant locket. "Come, Shannon," I said. "I must select my gown for dinner, and I'd like your help."

"Of course, Lady Beth," she replied.

But as soon as we were in my room, I said, "Gracious! Have you ever seen such a display!"

"I can't say that I have," Shannon said. "But I do feel sorry for her. I hope that her locket is found soon."

"But Shannon, she doesn't care for it at all," I said. "She said as much yesterday. And did you hear her? She's already scheming to get a fancier one!"

"It did seem that way," Shannon said uneasily. "But perhaps losing it has made Lady Gabrielle realize how much it truly means to her. After all, absence makes the heart grow fonder."

"Perhaps," I said doubtfully.

Just then, there was a knock at my door. It was

Mr. Harrison and Mrs. Morris. I had never seen them look so grave.

"Very sorry to disturb you, Lady Beth," Mr. Harrison said. "We'd like to have a word with Shannon. Is she here?"

"Of course," I said, opening the door wider so that they might enter.

But instead, Mrs. Morris said, "In your quarters, Shannon. At once."

Shannon glanced at me in confusion as she followed Mr. Harrison and Mrs. Morris. I followed too; after all, how could I stay behind?

"Pardon me," I said. "Is there a problem?"

Mr. Harrison cleared his throat. "Lady Beth, there is nothing for you to worry about," he said vaguely.

"I'd like to know what's going on," I said.

Mrs. Morris and Mr. Harrison exchanged a troubled look.

"If there is nothing for me to worry about, then it must be a trivial matter," I said. "In which case, I require Shannon's assistance now."

"Please, Lady Beth," Mrs. Morris spoke up. "It is not something we wish to bother you with."

"It's no bother."

"If you must know, Lady Beth, the Trufant locket has been found in Shannon's room," Mr. Harrison said.

Shannon gasped in surprise. "That's impossible!" she exclaimed. "Mr. Harrison, you must believe—"

"I have every hope that there is a reasonable explanation for this, but we must discuss the matter at once," he said, interrupting her. "I am sure you understand."

Oh, this was too much! That Gabrielle's hysterics could cast a bad light on Shannon!

"Shannon," I said. "Did you take the Trufant locket?"

"No, milady," she replied firmly.

"Very good, then," I said. "The locket is found, and no harm done. Now, if you'll excuse us—"

"I'm afraid it's not that simple, Lady Beth," Mrs. Morris said. "You see, the locket was discovered in a laundry basket of your clothes. Shannon is no longer responsible for the laundry. So we must also ask why there was a laundry basket in her room."

That sounded reasonable to me. "Go on, Shannon," I said. "Tell them why you had my laundry."

71

All the color drained from Shannon's face. She pressed her lips together and shook her head. "I am sorry, Lady Beth," she said. "But I cannot do that."

"Shannon! Don't be silly," I said. "Tell them why you have the laundry."

"I cannot," she repeated. "But I swear to you on my life that I did not steal the Trufant locket."

"Shannon, I implore you once more to tell us everything," Mr. Harrison said. "Otherwise, we will have no choice about how to proceed."

Shannon wiped a single tear from her cheek. "I understand," she said, her voice scarcely more than a whisper.

"Come, then," Mrs. Morris said, looking deeply disappointed as she took Shannon by the arm. "If you pack now, James can bring you to the station in time for the four o'clock train."

"Wait," I said. "Surely you're not—Shannon, *wait*—"

But Shannon didn't even look at me as Mrs. Morris led her away.

"Mr. Harrison!" I exclaimed. "What is the meaning of this? Why would James take Shannon to the train station?"

"Lady Beth," Mr. Harrison said. "You must understand the difficulty of this situation. I have no choice but to dismiss Shannon. How can I vouch for her innocence when she is hiding something from us?"

"I *know* that she did not take the Trufant locket," I said hotly. "And my parents will never let you dismiss an innocent person for a crime she didn't commit!"

I strode down the corridor and found my parents sitting together in the parlor. "A terrible injustice is under way!" I announced.

Mother glanced up from the letter she was writing. "Beth, my dear, whatever is the matter?" she asked.

"Mr. Harrison and Mrs. Morris have just dismissed Shannon," I said.

"We know, darling," Mother said. "Mr. Harrison told us that the Trufant locket was discovered in Shannon's room. I am sorry to hear that her guilt has been confirmed."

"But it hasn't been confirmed," I argued. "On the contrary, Shannon denies taking the locket. And I believe her."

"Well, I'm sure Mr. Harrison has his reasons,"

Father said, without even looking up from his newspaper.

"How can you say that?" I cried. "Shannon has done nothing wrong, and now she's out of a job—sent away from her home—"

Father finally looked at me. "Beth, Chatswood Manor is her place of employment first, and her home second," he said. "If Mr. Harrison sees fit to send her away, so be it. I trust his judgment, and to second-guess him would be out of line."

"I know you're fond of Shannon, Beth, but matters of staffing are the responsibility of Mr. Harrison," Mother said gently. "It is not our place to interfere."

A hard lump formed in my throat. "This is *wrong*," I choked out.

"My poor Beth," Mother said, her voice filled with sympathy. "I'm very sorry that something so unpleasant has happened on your birthday. Just put it from your mind."

"You don't understand—" I began.

"And I'll see to it that Miss Dalton helps with your toilette today and tomorrow," Mother promised. "I know how important your birthday festivities are, Beth. Don't worry, my darling; you'll look more beautiful than ever!"

I shook my head and turned away. Right then my birthday festivities didn't seem very important at all. Poor Shannon was being fired for something she didn't do. It was very clear to me that Mother and Father would not intervene on Shannon's behalf.

Which left me no choice but to do so myself.

From the parlor I went directly to the servants' staircase, but with every step, I felt the pangs of my conscience. My heart was pounding like it always did when I thought of disobeying Mother. I could still hear her advice: "Matters of staffing are the responsibility of Mr. Harrison. It is not our place to interfere."

And I was sure that in nearly every circumstance, Mother was right . . . but not today. Today, Shannon needed me. I was the only one who could help her. So I took a deep breath and hurried down the stairs before anyone saw me.

I found myself in a long corridor that was lined with dark-paneled doors. I pressed myself against the coarse wall beside the kitchen while I tried to determine where Mr. Harrison's quarters were located. The air was perfumed with the scent of cake, and I could hear a great deal of clanging and banging—no doubt Mrs. Beaudin and the kitchen staff were hard at work in preparation for tomorrow. I shook the thought from my head, though, for this was no time to be thinking about my birthday party. I had to find Mr. Harrison before Shannon finished packing her belongings and departed Chatswood Manor—forever.

But which one of the doors belonged to him? I had no choice but to try each one. At the first door, there was no answer. I stumbled into a bit of good fortune after I knocked at the second, for Mr. Harrison's deep voice carried through the door.

"Come in."

I slipped into his quarters and waited for him to look up from the ledger on his desk. When at last Mr. Harrison noticed me, he could not have been more surprised if His Royal Highness King George himself had appeared in the doorway.

"Lady Beth!" Mr. Harrison exclaimed. He rose at once, his eyes wide with alarm. "What are you doing here? What's happened? Has there been an accident?"

I shook my head. "No, not at all; everything is quite

all right," I replied. "I mean to say—no, things are *not* all right."

"Come," Mr. Harrison said, moving toward the door. "Allow me to escort you upstairs. We shall find your parents and—"

"Mr. Harrison, wait," I interrupted him. "I've come to speak with you about Shannon."

Mr. Harrison sighed. "Ah, yes—an unpleasant business. But you needn't worry, Lady Beth. I can assure you that Mrs. Morris will interview candidates to replace Shannon as soon as possible."

"That won't be necessary," I said. "You see, Shannon is innocent, so there is no reason to dismiss her or to look for a replacement."

A look of relief crossed Mr. Harrison's face.

"That is welcome news, indeed," he replied. "I thought it was unlikely that Shannon would do such a thing after two years at Chatswood Manor. In my experience, staff members given to petty thievery usually show their true character much sooner than that."

I clasped my hands together, delighted that Mr. Harrison understood. "Thank you, Mr. Harrison! Shannon will be overjoyed to learn she is still employed."

"I'm sure she will. Now, if you would just share the name of the guilty party, we can put this matter behind us," Mr. Harrison said.

My smiled faded. "I'm afraid I don't know who took Lady Gabrielle's locket," I replied. "But there is no doubt in my mind that Shannon is innocent."

"Lady Beth, all the evidence points to Shannon's guilt," Mr. Harrison said. "The stolen locket was found in her room. And Shannon herself was unwilling to explain why she had the laundry basket in the first place. Now, I will be more than happy to reinstate Shannon as your lady's maid. But first I need proof of her innocence."

"I don't have any proof . . . yet," I began. "But I'll find some, Mr. Harrison. I promise you. I won't give up until I've uncovered evidence that will—"

"*You?* Gathering evidence like a common detective?" Mr. Harrison exclaimed in shock. "No, no, Lady Beth, that would never do."

I opened my mouth to reply, but Mr. Harrison kept speaking.

"Your loyalty to Shannon does you credit. But as long as she is under a cloud of suspicion, there can be no employment for her at Chatswood Manor. Shannon is certainly not the first servant to be sent home in disgrace, nor will she be the last. The world is full of injustices, great and small."

My mind raced with worry. Surely there had to be a way to keep Shannon at Chatswood long enough for me to prove her innocence. But how could I convince Mr. Harrison to let her stay?

Then I remembered the demanding way in which Gabrielle spoke to servants. Such rudeness would not come easily to me, but I could at least try to imitate her forceful manner.

"Mr. Harrison, I *will* have Shannon here to do my hair for my birthday party tomorrow," I announced. "She is the *only* one at Chatswood who knows how to style it exactly as I want."

"Lady Beth, I must insist—"

"No, I must insist," I interrupted him.

Mr. Harrison looked at me intently for a long moment. "I will consider your request," he finally said. "More than that, I cannot promise."

Relief flooded my heart. "Oh, *thank you*, Mr. Harrison! Thank you!"

He crossed the room and led me back into the corridor. "And I trust, Lady Beth, that you will put the stolen locket out of your mind," he continued. "You should not trouble yourself with such matters. Nor should you be downstairs. If you return, I will have no choice but to inform your father. I know that he would be deeply displeased."

"I understand, Mr. Harrison."

"Now, run along and enjoy the rest of your birthday, Lady Beth."

"Yes, Mr. Harrison. I will."

As Mr. Harrison closed the door behind him, I heard a loud whisper.

"Lady Beth!"

I turned to find Shannon beckoning to me from another doorway. She pulled me into a whitewashed room equipped with a narrow bed, a washstand, and a simple chest of drawers. There was a half-packed valise on the foot of the bed.

"Shannon, is this your room?" I asked in astonishment, stunned by its plainness.

"Lady Beth, what are you doing down here?" she asked, ignoring my question. "I overheard Mr. Harrison.

You've got to get back upstairs before he leaves his quarters! Your father would—"

I shook my head. "Oh, Shannon, I don't care about that," I told her. "The important thing is that you're innocent—and I'm going to prove it. I've asked Mr. Harrison to let you stay to help me get ready for my birthday party, and we can use the time between now and then to clear your name."

"Lady Beth, you have a kind heart," Shannon said sadly. "And I do appreciate it. But I've accepted my fate. There is no choice for me but to leave Chatswood Manor."

"But where will you go?"

"Home, I suppose," Shannon said, holding the Saint Anthony medal between her fingers. "I won't be able to find another position in service. No one wants to hire a thief."

"Then how will you provide for yourself?"

Shannon didn't answer as she placed some folded handkerchiefs in her valise.

"You shall not be punished for a crime you didn't commit," I said firmly. "If you'd only tell me why you had the laundry basket in your room—"

"I cannot."

We stared at each other for a long moment. I could tell from the redness around Shannon's eyes that she had been crying.

"Please, Lady Beth," Shannon continued in a shaky voice. "Go upstairs. Enjoy your birthday. Don't give the Trufant locket—or me—another thought."

I grasped her hands in mine. "You'll see, Shannon," I promised. "I'll clear your name. I swear it."

I slipped out of Shannon's room and scurried upstairs as quickly as I could. After my conversation with Shannon, I was even more determined to find out the truth. I had made a promise to her—and I was going to do everything in my power to keep it.

8

*T*hough the scandal of the Gabrielle's locket hung over us like a heavy cloud, Shannon took extra pains with my toilette for my birthday dinner. After she helped me select a gown of midnight-blue silk adorned with tiny silver beads, she spent close to an hour brushing my hair. Then she pushed it back from my face with a blue velvet headband, and as a special finishing touch, she tucked an iridescent peacock feather behind my ear.

In the dining room, Cousin Gabrielle sat across from me. I noticed that she did not seem very pleased to be reunited with the Trufant locket, which gleamed around her neck. I was more suspicious than ever that she had been involved in its mysterious disappearance—but how could I find out for sure?

"You must be so relieved to have your locket back,"

I said pointedly. "I know that it's very dear to you."

"Yes," Gabrielle said. "I am sure that you are also relieved to know that your lady's maid is a thief and to have her out of your service before she stole from you as well."

Anger surged through me, but I remembered to keep my temper. If Gabrielle was indeed involved, I'd have to tread carefully to catch my cousin in a trap of her own making. I turned my attention to the other end of the table, where Uncle Claude was prattling on about his favorite subject.

"The signs are clear," Uncle Claude said. "Answer me this: Why would the Germans spend so much on their military if they weren't preparing for aggression? If Kaiser Wilhelm isn't a warmonger, he has a strange way of showing it."

"I will grant you that," Father conceded. "Perhaps he wants to be prepared for any future conflicts, now that France and Russia have formed an alliance."

Uncle Claude seemed offended. "We have no choice but to become allies!" he exclaimed. "It would be a scandal to sit by, unprepared, while our neighbors assemble an army on our doorstep."

"You know, there are scandals closer to home that are just as captivating," I spoke up.

All eyes turned to me. My mouth was suddenly so dry that I could barely speak, but I forced myself to go on.

"For example, this scandal involving my lady's maid, Shannon. A kinder, more loyal soul you'll never meet. And yet *someone* saw fit to frame her for a crime she didn't commit."

Across from me, Gabrielle dropped her fork. It clattered on her plate.

"Beth," Mother said in her warning voice.

But I pressed on. "Who would do such a thing?" I continued. "Another staff member? Or perhaps one of our many visitors?"

A rapid stream of French spewed from Uncle Claude; Father spoke at the same time.

"Young lady, your mother and I specifically told you that this matter is not your concern," he said sternly.

"On the contrary, Father, it concerns us all," I said as politely as I could. "If Shannon didn't take the locket, as she claims, then someone else must have. And if that someone—a *thief*, I might add—remains under the roof of Chatswood Manor—"

Gabrielle suddenly put her hands to her head. "*Maman*, I am unwell," she said in a trembling voice. "I wish to lie down at once."

Across the room, Mr. Harrison discreetly rang for Helena. She appeared in the doorway a moment later.

"Beth, you have upset your cousin," Aunt Beatrice said. "She already succumbed to a sick-headache this afternoon, and I can tell from her pale color that it has returned."

"But isn't it more upsetting to think that a thief walks free through the halls of Chatswood Manor?" I pressed on. My eyes followed Helena as she hurried to Gabrielle's side. "That there could be a thief among us, right here in this very room?"

Helena jolted when I spoke—and overturned a crystal pitcher of water! Ice and lemon slices tumbled across the table as water soaked the tablecloth.

"Clumsy!" Gabrielle shouted as she backed away from the table so that the water wouldn't touch her gown. But in the process, Gabrielle knocked over her chair, which landed on Bertram's foot!

"Ow!" he yelped before clasping his hands over his mouth. In his haste to move away from Gabrielle's chair, Bertram then slammed into the table!

"Mind the candles!" Mother cried.

Mr. Harrison leaped forward to steady the trembling candelabra. At the same moment, he managed to cover the water stain with a large cloth.

"If this is how you Brits manage something so simple as a family dinner, perhaps you'd best stay out of the war," Uncle Claude barked.

"I am very sorry, Lady Gabrielle," Helena muttered.

"You ought to mind your pointy elbows, you oaf!" Gabrielle snapped.

"Gabrielle!" Aunt Beatrice said reprovingly.

"Oh, *ma tête*," Gabrielle moaned, burrowing her head in her hands. The anger on Aunt Beatrice's face was immediately replaced with concern.

"Helena, take Gabrielle to her room," Aunt Beatrice ordered. "Make sure she has anything she desires."

"Of course, *madame*," Helena said as she guided Gabrielle from the room.

The flurry of activity continued as Bertram and the other footmen cleared the mess from the table.

"Lady Beth, I sincerely apologize for this dreadful chain of events," Mr. Harrison said. "We will do everything in our power to restore dignity to your birthday dinner."

"Mr. Harrison, it is quite all right," I said, grinning as I watched the spectacle going on around me. Indeed, I couldn't be happier. It was clear to me that Gabrielle and Helena were hiding something about the disappearance of the Trufant locket. Now I had no doubt that exposing their secret would be the key to saving Shannon's position.

As soon as dinner was over, I excused myself from the table. I just had to tell Shannon about Gabrielle and Helena's strange behavior—even if it meant sneaking downstairs for the second time in one day.

I hurried down the stairs as quietly as I could, glancing behind me more than once to make sure that I was alone. If I were discovered downstairs again, Mr. Harrison would surely tell my parents, which would make it impossible to solve this mystery before Shannon's time ran out.

I knocked on Shannon's door, holding my breath until she opened it. Her eyes grew wide with surprise. "Lady Beth! Again!" she said as she pulled me into her room. "What are you doing here?"

"So much happened at dinner tonight!" I said glee-fully. "Just wait till you hear!"

Shannon listened attentively while I told her all about Gabrielle's and Helena's behavior.

"I agree that it does sound very odd," she finally said. "But please don't get your hopes up too high, Lady Beth. There is still no proof that they are involved."

"There's no proof *yet*," I corrected her. "But tomor-row, I'll find some. I swear it!"

Then I noticed that Shannon's valise, still neatly packed, was waiting by the door. "Shannon," I began. "What—are you—"

She seemed to understand what I was trying to say. "Mr. Harrison said he would make a decision about my departure tonight," Shannon said in a quiet voice. "I expect that he or Mrs. Morris will be along directly to tell me. So I—I thought it best to be ready to leave at once."

My heart clenched. "Oh, Shannon, I'm sure he'll let you stay through the party tomorrow!" I told her. "Oh, he must—"

"Shh!" Shannon said suddenly.

I listened carefully, but I didn't hear anything except the jangle of Mrs. Morris's keys.

Mrs. Morris's keys!

If she were on her way to Shannon's room—

If she discovered me down here—

Shannon shook her head, warning me not to make a sound. Then she grabbed a candle in one hand and pulled me into the hallway.

"There's a passage over here," Shannon said in a rushed whisper as she led me around the corner. "Walk forward for a hundred yards—"

"A passage?" I repeated.

"Hidden, in the wall," Shannon said softly in my ear. "It's safe. Dark, though. You'll want to watch your step. The candle will help. There will be a door—"

"Has anyone seen Shannon?" Mrs. Morris's voice carried down the corridor.

Shannon tapped on a spot in the wall. To my amazement, a door sprung open where no door had been before!

"Is that—"

Shannon didn't wait for me to finish my question. "Go!" she whispered urgently as she placed the candle

in my hand and pushed me through the doorway.

The last thing I heard was Shannon saying, quite clearly, "Yes, Mrs. Morris, I'm on my way."

Then she pulled the secret door closed, leaving me alone in the dark.

9

$\mathcal{I}$'d never been somewhere so dark in all my life. The faint halo of light from the candle cast creeping shadows around me, but it didn't help illuminate my path.

I took a deep breath to steady my nerves. *Shannon wouldn't send me somewhere unsafe*, I reminded myself. *If I've ever trusted Shannon before, I've got to trust her now.*

My fingers were trembling as I reached for the wall. The stone was damp and cold. My hand recoiled, but I forced myself to hold on. I needed the wall as my guide to know where I stepped. Anything, really, could be hiding within this darkness. Rats. Spiders. Things that should never see the light of day.

I shuddered in spite of myself. The sooner I was out of this passage, the better. The passage wound this way and that, but I carefully moved forward, step by step. I tried to be brave—I tried as hard as I could—but being alone in the dark was one of the most terrifying things I had ever experienced.

If Mrs. Morris sends Shannon away tonight—
If the candle extinguishes—
If I lose my way in the blackness—
And no one knows where I am—

Would I ever find my way out?

I strained my ears, listening for any sound that might tell me where I was—the rumble of Father's and Uncle Claude's voices as they chatted in the smoking room; the clanging of the flues as the housemaids lit the evening fires; the splashing of suds as the scullery maids scoured pots and pans. But the thick stone walls made the tunnel soundproof; I could hear nothing.

Suddenly, my fingers slipped into a crevice within the wall. It must have been a place where the mortar between two stones had begun to crumble. The space was narrow, scarcely wider than my fingers. I felt a smattering of gritty dust . . . the sticky threads of a cobweb . . .

The binding of a book . . .

A book!

94

My heart started pounding as I grasped the book between two fingers and gently eased it out of the crack. Who would hide a book in this secret passageway?

I held the book close to my candle and peered at its tattered leather cover, which had been warped by dampness. The pages were slightly stuck together but otherwise appeared to be intact.

Suddenly I was struck by an astonishing thought: Could this be the missing journal of Great-Grandmother Elizabeth? I squinted at the spidery handwriting on the page. But the passageway was too dark; I couldn't read a single word.

I was so eager to examine the book in better light that I forgot how scared I'd been just moments before. I started to run through the rest of the passageway. When the path began to slope upward, I slowed my step so that I wouldn't miss the door that Shannon had mentioned. Then my fingers brushed against what felt like a wooden frame. I paused and held the candle as closely as I dared.

Yes. There was a tiny door tucked into the wall.

I pressed my ear to the door and listened closely. Oh, if only Shannon had told me *where* in the house this passage would take me! What if I opened this door and burst in on Father and Uncle Claude in the smoking room? Or Mother and Aunt Beatrice in the parlor? How on earth would I explain why I was scurrying through the walls of Chatswood Manor like a mouse?

Several long, slow minutes ticked by. At last, I took a deep breath and eased the door open. Then I stepped, blinking from the brightness . . . into the library!

I laughed aloud in relief. I should've known that Shannon would make sure I found my way to an empty room—and indeed, even with a house full of visitors, the library got precious little use because Chatswood had so many other rooms to gather in. I tucked the book under my arm and escaped to my bedroom, where I found Shannon waiting for me with my nightly tray of drinking chocolate and biscuits.

"Oh, good, you found your way!" she cried. "I was worried, Lady Beth. I thought perhaps I ought to go in after you."

"Shannon! You're still here!" I exclaimed, just as happy to see her as she was to see me. "I was so afraid that Mrs. Morris would send you away."

Shannon shook her head. "No, milady—or perhaps

I should say not yet," she replied. "Mr. Harrison has decided that I may stay on through tomorrow, in order to help you get ready for your birthday party."

"That's splendid news!" I said happily.

"And"—Shannon leaned closer to me, lowering her voice—"Mrs. Morris said that he changed his mind quite suddenly, during the course of dinner."

I gasped. "So Mr. Harrison noticed how strangely Gabrielle and Helena behaved, too! Oh, Shannon, he knows you're innocent! And so he's giving me time to clear your name!"

"Well, I don't know about all that," Shannon said. "I'm just glad to help you through tomorrow. Here, milady, let me take the candle from you. And what's this under your arm?"

I didn't want to tell Shannon about the book. Not yet anyway. Not until I knew what it was. So I tossed it on my bedside table and said, "Just a volume of poetry I found in the library after I exited the secret passageway—a little something to read before bed. I'd like to change into my nightgown now, please."

"The blue one is ready, Lady Beth."

"Thank you," I said as I examined it. "Shannon, I

see no trace of the stain you mentioned. Where was it?"

"I'll not tell," Shannon said playfully. "I'm ever so glad that it finally succumbed to my efforts. I've never met a more stubborn stain."

"You're a fine one for keeping secrets after all," I told her as Shannon began to unbutton my gown.

When I was ready for bed, I bade Shannon good night. Alone at last, I sipped my drinking chocolate and started to read.

Tis so cold tonight that I am writing with gloved hands, longing to huddle under my blankets. But since the girls have taken such pains to teach me to read and write, a little practice before bed is the least I can do. I'll need to find a good place to hide this journal. I suspect that Nancy takes liberties with my side of the room. Nothing I own is safe from her prying eyes, and what Nancy knows, the rest of the house soon knows, too. And I can't imagine that the family would look kindly on me keeping a journal, even though I keep it for only myself.

I squinted at the page in confusion. Could this have been written by Elizabeth? But who was Nancy? Elizabeth would've shared her room with *Katherine*— if she shared a room at all. And I couldn't imagine that any of the Chatswoods would've been upset about Elizabeth keeping a journal. Was it possible this journal belonged to someone other than my great-grandmother? I decided to keep reading.

A lovely day with the girls was ruined by the events at tea this afternoon. Mildred, the newest housemaid, took more than her fair share of toast, and Emily decided that she would be punished for it. The housemaids have locked her in the basement for the whole night, with orders to launder every piece of linen the family has dirtied! It was an ugly scene, Mildred shaking and crying as they shut the door to the basement and bolted it. When it was time to retire, she was very much on my mind, but I knew that I mustn't enter the basement or I'd face Emily's wrath as well. I slipped through one of the under-passages so that I might see for myself how Mildred fared. She did not expect to see me—she doesn't yet know about all that hides within these walls—and I nearly frightened her half to death, poor girl. It took a great deal of convincing before she believed that I truly was Essie Bridges and not some ghost come to torment her. Of course that nasty Gertie has filled her head with frightful stories about this house and its past. But I reassured Mildred that there's no such thing as ghosts, and I left her with a few extra candles and a pot of chamomile tea to soothe her nerves as she worked. I'm glad that a housemaid's life is not my lot, but I can't stop thinking of poor Mildred. Now, safe in my room, I am full of regret that I didn't do more for her.

A wave of disappointment washed over me. So the journal hadn't belonged to Elizabeth after all. But the more I thought about what I read, the less disappointed I felt. After all, this journal was still an exciting secret

I had discovered! Who was this Essie Bridges? She must've been a servant at Chatswood—but when? A quick glance through the rest of the journal revealed that it didn't have any dates written in it. What was Essie's role, if not housemaid? A lady's maid? A kitchen maid? A scullery maid? Who were "the girls"—other servants? Or maybe her daughters?

And what did she mean by "all that hides within these walls"? Were there even more secret passages? Or perhaps something else entirely?

There was only one way to find out.

I nibbled one of the biscuits Shannon had brought me and made sure that there was an extra candle at my bedside. Essie's writing was faint and hard to read, so the night ahead of me would be a long one. But I was determined to stay up as late as possible; I wanted to devour every page of the secret journal.

10

When I awoke the next morning, sunlight was streaming through my windows. I had stayed up very late reading, and it took me a moment before I suddenly remembered: my birthday party! It was just hours away! There was surely a whirlwind of activity downstairs, and no doubt Shannon would be along shortly to get me ready for the day, but until then....

I reached for Essie's journal.

What a happy Christmas the girls had! Their mother outdid herself in selecting their presents: lovely boots with bright shining buttons, velvet and satin hair ribbons, and a book of verses with beautiful pictures in it. And there was one special gift for each girl. Sparrow received a new paint set with a wonderful assortment of colors and three fine brushes, while Lark was given a bottle of India ink and a leather book comprised of blank pages. I know the girls will spend many hours quietly absorbed in these pastimes through the cold winter ahead. I was very grateful for my own gifts: a new apron, a brush-and-comb set, and a packet of fine, sharp needles for mending. I'll surely put those to good use!

A knock at my door forced me to shove the journal under my pillow.

"Still abed, milady?" Shannon asked as she entered my room. "Did you stay up too late reading?"

"Reading?" I repeated, trying not to sound too alarmed. How did Shannon know about Essie's journal?

"The volume of poems from the library, milady."

"Oh, yes," I said, relieved. "Yes, I suppose I did stay up rather late."

"Today will be a busy one, Lady Beth," Shannon continued. "All the house is in a tizzy preparing for your birthday party. I daresay that you'll be so worn out

from dancing tonight that you'll be fast asleep before
your head touches the pillow!"

I simply smiled as I slipped out of bed so that
Shannon could begin my toilette. It *was* going to be a
busy day for me.

But not in the way that Shannon expected.

The housemaids always tidied the upstairs bedrooms
after breakfast, so I knew there would be no way for
me to read more of Essie's journal in private. Instead,
I decided to go downstairs to see what else I could
discover about the mystery of the Trufant locket.

Through an open door on the side of the house, I
spotted James, the chauffeur, who was crouched down
polishing the motorcar. And best of all, he was alone.

"Hello, James," I said as I approached.

James was startled by my voice. When he realized who had addressed him, he scrambled to his feet.
"Lady Beth!" he exclaimed. "What are you—beg pardon, what can I do for you? Did you, ah, are you going
somewhere?"

"No, not today," I replied. "I was hoping that I
might have a word."

"With me?" James asked, looking even more confused.

"Yes. It's about Shannon."

At that, James nodded knowingly. "What a bad business," he said sadly. "She ought not to be dismissed, Lady Beth, if you don't mind my speaking plain."

"Not at all, James. I agree with you. I think that Shannon's been framed," I confided.

James leaned against the motorcar as I spoke, staring at me intently. The more I told him, the darker his eyes grew, until he looked as serious and handsome as a hero from a novel. It's no wonder that I've heard Jennie and Nora giggling just because he tipped his cap to them.

"Well, I'll be honest with you, Lady Beth," James finally said. "I'm *certain* that Shannon is innocent. She's always been a good one. Not like some of them wretched housemaids—always full of mean-spirited gossip, with nary a kind word."

"Is that so?" I asked.

"You can count on it," James told me. "They stop right quick when I'm around, but I've heard enough to know that most of them plumb hate one another."

"Do you think one of the housemaids stole the Trufant locket?" I asked eagerly—perhaps *too* eagerly. For James immediately lifted his hands and said, "Now, now, that's not what I meant. Chatswood Manor is not a house that employs people of low character. We haven't had a theft here since long before my time."

"So if it's not one of our staff," I said slowly, "then it *must* be Lady Gabrielle and Helena."

"I can't speak ill of Lady Gabrielle," James said firmly. "It's not my place, and besides I don't know her a whit. But I *can* tell you my impression of that Helena—she's an odd bird."

"Go on," I encouraged him.

"It was the night the Trufants arrived," he began. "At first I felt a bit of pity for Helena. We could all see that Lady Gabrielle was running her ragged, and you could tell just from the sight of her that Helena was exhausted. So Helena missed the servants' meal, and by the time she finally came down for a bite to eat, Mrs. Beaudin was in bed. Now, I don't know how they do it in France, but Helena marched herself right into the kitchen and started eating the biscuits that Mrs. Beaudin had fixed for your birthday picnic."

"Did she really? She *ate* them?"

"Aye, she did. I saw it with my own eyes—she stood there at the counter pushing them in her mouth faster than she could breathe. And it was wrong for her to do that! On your first day of service you learn that there's food for the family and there's food for the staff, and the two are not the same. But I still felt sorry for her. She must've been awfully hungry to do such a thing."

I was quiet for a moment. It had never occurred to me that the staff might work so hard that they were forced to skip meals. Or that they had to eat different food than the family. I had always assumed they ate the same delicious food we did.

"As it turns out, Mr. Harrison was making his nightly rounds before retiring, and he almost caught Helena in the act! But wouldn't you know, that Helena is a sly one. She simply brushed the crumbs from her apron and said that she had served the biscuits to Lady Gabrielle, and that she always had a plate of biscuits before bed."

"But Gabrielle has *strawberries* before bed. I heard Helena tell Mrs. Morris on the day they arrived. So . . . she *lied* to Mr. Harrison? Just like that?"

"That she did. And I made a note to myself—I thought, James, don't be trusting that one. Anyone who lies that easily—and that quickly—is not to be trusted!"

A brief surge of anger swelled in me—oh, that Helena! Lying to Mr. Harrison—on her first day at Chatswood Manor! Now there was no doubt in my mind that she was involved in the disappearance of the Trufant locket. But why? And even more important—how would I prove it?

"James, will you help me?" I asked urgently. "Will you help me clear Shannon's name?"

A troubled expression clouded his eyes. "I don't know, Lady Beth. I need to keep my position here. My mum depends on me to send my pay home to care for the little ones—my brothers and sisters."

Then James sighed. "But I like Shannon, and it's not right what's been done to her. So I'll do everything I can, Lady Beth. And that's a promise."

"James!"

Mr. Harrison's voice rang across the courtyard.

James and I both jumped up, looking as guilty as though *we'd* been the ones stealing biscuits.

"I'll thank *you* to tend to your duties, James," Mr. Harrison said sternly. Then, without a word to me, he led me back into the house. I didn't even have a chance to thank James—or to apologize for getting him in trouble.

"Lady Beth, I thought that I made myself perfectly clear yesterday," Mr. Harrison said. "The downstairs is no place for you. Do you understand?"

"But, Mr. Harrison, I just want—"

"No, milady, I cannot indulge this reckless behavior. It's not right for the staff to see you downstairs. It upsets the natural order of things."

Two shameful red circles burned on my cheeks. How foolish I had been to think that Mr. Harrison had noticed Gabby's and Helena's strange behavior at dinner last night. How foolish to think that he was on my side. All he cared about was appearances and which part of the house I stayed in.

Of course I understood my place at Chatswood Manor. How could I not? It had been drilled into me by Mother, by Father, by my nannies and governesses ever since I was small. I knew that everyone at Chatswood—everyone in our village, actually—would someday look to me for guidance. But this was different. Shannon's future was at stake—and it was up to me to do something about it! Wasn't that so much more important than following some silly rules about where it was proper for me to go and where it wasn't?

"Yes, Mr. Harrison. I understand," I said stiffly as we reached the top of the stairs.

"Very good, Lady Beth. I bid you good day," he replied with a curt nod of his head.

Frustration welled inside of me as I watched Mr. Harrison retreat. I was beginning to lose hope that Shannon would tell me why she had the laundry basket. If I could only discover the answer, I felt confident that Mr. Harrison would let her stay—permanently. Perhaps the housemaids could help me. Since the laundry was their responsibility, they might know why a basket had been found in Shannon's room.

I stood alone, lost in thought. Mr. Harrison had told me that I could not go downstairs. But he had said nothing about questioning the staff *upstairs*!

The upper floors of Chatswood Manor were buzzing with activity as the housemaids hurried around.

I knew I would find most of them in the ballroom, decorating for my birthday party. Sure enough, as I approached the ballroom, I could hear voices. It sounded like Nora and Jennie. I paused outside the door to listen.

"Steady, now," Nora said. "Don't bruise the blossoms!"

"This is too much work for two people," complained Jennie. "*Where* are May and Peggy? A fine time to leave us with all of this to take care of, with the birthday party just hours away!"

"Well, now, you can't very well blame them," Nora said. She sounded as if she had been holding on to a morsel of scandalous gossip. "After the scene in the basement this morning."

I heard Jennie suck in her breath. "Go on. Go on!"

"Someone has been throwing *garbage* down the *laundry chutes!*" Nora said gleefully.

"Well, I never!" exclaimed Jennie. "Who would do such a thing?"

"I'm sure that *I* don't know," Nora replied. "Though Mrs. Beaudin says it's the custom in France to have *garbage* chutes in the walls."

"Filthy!" Jennie said with a contemptuous sniff.

"And what a dreadful mess it made—in every single basket, too! Now poor Peggy and May are down there picking garbage out of the laundry, searching for new stains on the linens—oh, they've got their work cut out for them, and I don't envy them one bit."

"Better them than us," Jennie said as she and Nora left the ballroom. They stopped suddenly when they saw me.

"Oh, Jennie, here you are," I said, as though I'd been looking for her. "Might I have a word?"

"Of course, milady, but I'm really very busy," she said. Jennie watched Nora continue down the hall, as if she wished that she had been so lucky.

"I want to ask you about the laundry."

"The laundry?"

"Yes, the laundry. I was wondering if you knew why Shannon had a laundry basket in her room yesterday."

Jennie didn't meet my eyes. "Oh, milady, I'll be in for such a tongue-lashing if I don't help Nora bring in more garlands!"

"Then I'll walk with you," I said. "You see, I've got

to find out what really happened to the Trufant locket. Come, we'll go to the garden together and chat along the way. I suppose I could even help you hang the garlands, if it would ease your burden."

"No, no, that would never do!" a creaky voice spoke up.

"Great-Grandmother Cecily," I said in surprise as she approached us.

"The birthday girl can't go into the ballroom before her party begins," Cecily said firmly. "It would ruin the surprise!"

Then Cecily swatted at Jennie's arm and said, "Run along, now. You've more important things to do than gab in the corridor."

Jennie curtsied and hurried on. I couldn't help but notice that she seemed tremendously relieved to get away.

Then Cecily slipped her arm through mine. "Come now, Beth; bring me to the parlor," she ordered. "I would like to sit by the fire. You can keep me company."

I forced myself to smile and nod, though what I really wanted to do was run after Jennie and finish asking her questions.

"Yes, Great-Grandmother," I said dutifully.

In the parlor, Cecily settled herself on the couch beside the Chinese lacquer cabinet and patted the cushion beside her. "Sit. That's a good girl," she said. "Now, tell me why you were badgering that poor maid."

"I wasn't badgering her," I replied. "I just wanted to ask her some questions. I think that Shannon has been unfairly accused of taking Cousin Gabrielle's locket, and I want to find the real thief."

"Oh, yes, quite right," Cecily said. "I agree."

My mouth dropped open. "You *do*?" I exclaimed.

Cecily nodded vigorously. "Yes, yes, I am sure of it."

"How do you know, Great-Grandmother?"

Cecily blinked a few times before she answered. "Know what?"

"Know that Shannon is innocent?"

"Shannon? Who is Shannon?"

I took a deep breath and tried to stay calm. "We were talking about Gabrielle's locket," I began.

"Oh, yes, the one that was stolen," Cecily remembered. "She's lucky that she got it back, my dear. When Elizabeth's chatelaine disappeared, it was never seen again."

Now *I* was confused. "What chatelaine?"

"Elizabeth had a chatelaine, and she wore it always," Cecily said. "She loved it so. She pinned it to the front of her dress, a beautiful silver brooch with trinkets attached—I recall a tiny notebook and pencil, a paint box, a tear-catcher, which I'm sure she filled to the brim after Lady Mary's passing. You could always hear Elizabeth approach. Her chatelaine announced her by chiming like tiny bells."

"What happened to it?"

"One day it just . . . vanished. It was right after Elizabeth married Maxwell, so perhaps she felt that as a married woman she'd have no more time for such indulgences—though we were all very sad to see her give up her paints. She was very talented, you know. And, now that I think on it, the chatelaine disappeared after Katherine departed for America. So perhaps Elizabeth took it off since there would be no more long afternoons painting in the garden whilst Katherine composed her verses."

"But I thought Elizabeth was the poet, not Katherine," I said in confusion.

"Isn't that what I said?" Cecily retorted, leaving

me even more perplexed; perhaps I had misheard her. "Either way, Elizabeth removed her chatelaine, and it was never seen again."

"Was there an investigation? Were the staff quarters searched as they were when Gabrielle's locket went missing?"

Cecily shook her head. "No. Nothing like that. The staff at Chatswood loved Lady Elizabeth, and no one would have stolen a thing from her. No, she seemed quite content to pretend that it had never existed. But you can see it there in the portrait. Like I said, she wore it always. Until suddenly she didn't."

"How strange," I said.

Cecily smiled knowingly. "Chatswood Manor has always been a place where secrets are born," she said. "And it's where they're buried, too—never to be spoken of again."

"Secrets? *What* secrets?" I asked eagerly.

Cecily gave me a sharp look. Then she stifled a yawn and said, "Run along and leave an old woman to her thoughts, dear. Don't bother the staff with silly questions; it's not your place. And ring for the girl on your way out, please. I should like a spot of tea."

"Yes, Great-Grandmother," I said, trying not to sigh as I rose. I should've expected her swift dismissal. After all, that was how it always went: The more questions I had, the harder it was to find their answers.

11

After lunch, Mother told me to rest in advance of my birthday party. I am sure she expected me to sleep, but how could I? I decided that lying on the bed, quietly reading Essie's journal, would have to do.

Returned late last night from a trip to London with the family. Such an adventure it was! My eyes scarcely knew where to look first—the streets crowded with people, the horses on the cobblestones pulling carriages and buses, the buildings and bell towers crowding the streets. And my! How people stared at the girls—as if they'd never seen a set of twins before. Of course, I know the girls are quite a sight, being as nearly identical as they are. Though I can always tell the girls apart—I'd

be a poor excuse for a lady's maid if I couldn't—
most who meet them cannot. It's little wonder
that Sparrow always wears red, while Lark insists
on dressing in blue. I daresay it helps everyone
else to tell them apart, even their father! Not
that their mother needs to rely on their clothes.
She knows her girls the way only a mother does.

I gasped out loud. *Twins! Twins named Lark and Sparrow!* But there had only ever been one set of twins at Chatswood: Elizabeth and Katherine. I was sure of that much. So it stood to reason that Essie Bridges was talking about Elizabeth and Katherine. She must have been their ladies' maid. All her stories about "the girls" were actually stories about my own great-grandmother and her sister! *The hands that wrote these words brushed Elizabeth's hair,* I thought. *They tied Katherine's sash.*

Then I frowned. *But why did Essie call them Lark and Sparrow?* I wondered. Were they nicknames . . . or something more? My mind raced as I pondered this. Perhaps they were code names Essie used, to protect herself in case it was discovered that she was keeping a journal about the family. Surely that would have been frowned upon. But how would *I* find out which one was which? Though I wasn't even halfway through, I decided to read the journal over again from the very beginning in case there were clues I had missed.

Just then there was a knock at my door. It was Shannon, and her face was shining with excitement.

"Excuse the interruption, Lady Beth," she began. "But Lady Liz sent me. She says it's time to get ready for your birthday party!"

"Already?" I exclaimed as my heart started pounding.

"I've drawn your bath," she continued. "It's piping hot, and I used the perfumed oils your father brought from London. Lady Liz told me I might. After all, tonight will be the most special night of your life, Lady Beth. And it begins right now!"

After a long soak in the violet-scented water, I returned to my room. Sitting at the dressing table, I closed my eyes while Shannon arranged my hair.

"You know, Shannon," I said. "I've been wondering about something."

"Yes, milady?"

"If laundry duty is the worst of all the housemaid's chores, why did you still have a laundry basket after you became a lady's maid?"

Shannon sighed, ever so softly. "Lady Beth, as I have already said—"

"I want to help you," I interrupted her. "That's all. If you would just tell me—I'm sure that whatever the reason is, it can't be that bad—"

"If I could tell you, I would," she said, her voice full of sorrow.

We were quiet while Shannon helped me into my gown. Then she stood back to look at me, her hands pressed to her heart.

"Oh, Lady Beth," Shannon breathed. "You are a vision."

I hardly recognized my own reflection in the full-length mirror. My silk gown was as blue as the larkspur that grew in the garden, with a gossamer overskirt the color of sunlight at dawn. Whenever I moved, it shimmered as though stardust had been woven into the delicate tulle. The finest lace peeked out from under my hems. Satin gloves, the same shade as my dress, stretched to my elbows. And my hair—oh, my hair! Shannon had carefully arranged it into waves around my face, with beautiful curls flowing down my back. She had also woven a golden tiara through it, which reflected the light like a halo. It was the most grown-up hairstyle I'd ever worn. Of course, I couldn't wear my hair all the way up. Not yet, anyway. Not until I was ready for marriage—and I wouldn't be, not for at least five or six more years.

Of course, the most beautiful part of my costume was the Elizabeth necklace, nestled against my heart. *Did Elizabeth stand here once?* I wondered. *Did she look at her reflection in this very same mirror? Did she, too, feel the weight of the Elizabeth necklace round her neck, and know—body and soul—just how much it signified?*

"Lady Beth?" Shannon's gentle voice interrupted my thoughts. "They're waiting for you."

My pulse quickened. "It's time, then?"

"It is."

Shannon and I walked down the corridor in silence. With every step, my nerves jangled. I had never been the guest of honor at a ball before—not in my whole life! All those eyes would be watching me, all night long—when I walked, when I talked, when I danced, when I ate. What if I stumbled on the stairs? What if I spilled my cake? What if I tripped during a waltz? If I should make a mistake—in front of all those eyes—

Just before we reached the staircase, Shannon held me back. She stared at me with a critical eye, fluffing my skirt, straightening the tiara, and adjusting the Elizabeth necklace.

"You look exquisite," she finally whispered.

"Shannon? I'm not—"

"Of course you are," Shannon replied, as if she already knew what I wanted to say. She took my hands in hers and squeezed them. "You've been preparing for this moment all your life. And you'll be perfect. I know it. Now, go, Lady Beth. The party can't begin without you!"

Shannon's reassuring words were just what I needed to hear. "Thank you," I whispered as my dread melted away.

She simply smiled and nodded, then stepped back. I took a deep breath and continued on alone. I could hear a few faint strains of music coming from below.

At the top of the stairs, I was nearly blinded by the chandeliers all ablaze, their light glittering off the crystal. I turned my head for one last look at Shannon. I could hardly see her, she was so hidden by the shadows. But it was enough to know that she was there.

I took another deep breath.

And I started my descent.

Slowly, slowly, one step at a time. My gloved hand rested ever so lightly on the polished banister. I smiled the way Mother had showed me: just enough so that my lips were barely parted, and not so much that my nose crinkled. I remembered what Mother had told me: "Enter slowly, my dear, as you should rush for no one. Take your time so that the whole room may gaze on you and admire your loveliness."

Time stopped—no, *everything* stopped! The music, the dancing, the chatter, all of it ceased as my family and the guests turned to look at me. I smiled into a sea of faces: There was Cecily standing beside Grandmother Eliza; Uncle Claude and Aunt Beatrice flanking a sullen Gabrielle. Lord and Lady Everheart by the balcony; Sir Edgar and Lady Jessamine; my maiden aunts clustered around a table filled with sweets. And then, to my delight, I saw Mother and Father waiting for me at the foot of the stairs! Ten more steps—five more—two more—one. I had made it to the ballroom.

Mother embraced me first. "Perfect," she whispered near my ear.

Then Father offered me his arm and whisked me into the middle of the ballroom. The orchestra immediately began to play another waltz. Father and I twirled around and around until I felt as though I were flying!

"Remember when you were small, Beth?" he asked. "And I'd hold you over my head and spin until you screamed with delight? And the instant I put you down, you'd beg for more?"

"Yes!" I said, laughing. "What a little goose I was!"

"I'm not so certain of that," Father replied. "Because all I see before me is the most beautiful swan."

When the waltz ended, the orchestra struck up another, and Uncle Claude was waiting to whirl me around the room. Then Cousin Edward from London, followed by Lord Wright, and then my uncle Michael. After that, I was quite tired out! But there was no time to rest, for Mr. Harrison beckoned to me; it was time for the presentation of the birthday cake. Everyone in the ballroom gasped as the footmen wheeled it in on a trolley. Mrs. Beaudin had outdone herself! Candied violets cascaded down the five-tier cake, with twelve shimmering candles flickering on the top layer. My face was flushed from dancing and delight as everyone sang "Happy Birthday." Then Mr. Harrison gave me an elegant knife with a mother-of-pearl handle. The cake was far too beautiful to eat, let alone cut, and I felt sorry about slicing it. But oh! my surprise when I realized that it was filled with berries and whipped cream!

I decided to eat my piece of cake on the balcony. It felt good to stand outside, where a gentle breeze cooled my cheeks. Overhead, the stars twinkled merrily, as if they, too, were celebrating. The night was rich with the sounds of summer: I heard the crickets singing, the tree frogs peeping, the purr of the motorcar's engine.

Wait. Why did James have the motorcar out? Was someone ill? No, if James had been to fetch the doctor, he would have brought him to the front of the house. Was there some sort of emergency? I glanced behind me. No, there stood Mr. Harrison, attending to all the business of the party. Then what was James doing, driving round to the servants' entrance?

Suddenly, I realized just what he must be doing. "Oh no," I whispered in horror. "Shannon!"

A wave of shame washed over me. Since the party had started, I hadn't given Shannon a single thought. No, I'd danced and laughed and smiled and eaten cake, and forgotten all about the plight of my lady's maid and friend. And now, at this very moment, James was preparing to take her to the train station— I just knew it!

I strode through the ballroom as quickly as I could, trying to be gracious as one guest after another wished me a happy birthday. I could not appear as if anything was troubling me, but I also could not afford to waste time exchanging pleasantries. Time was of the essence, and I had to keep my promise to Shannon.

"Oh, there you are, Cousin," Gabrielle said. She raised her glass of cordial to me. "Lovely party, isn't it? You certainly look to be enjoying yourself. Shall I send Helena for some blotting papers? Your face is terribly shiny."

"No, thank you," I said shortly as I hurried away.

When I reached the corridor, I broke into a run

and didn't stop until I had nearly flown to the court-yard—where I found James putting Shannon's small valise into the motorcar.

"James!" I gasped, trying to catch my breath. "You— you promised!"

His dark eyes were sorrowful. "'Tis Mr. Harrison's orders, milady," he said simply. "I've no choice."

I pounded on the motorcar's sleek window. "Shannon!" I cried. "Come out!"

She opened the door a crack. "I'm sorry that I didn't have a chance to say good-bye," she whispered hoarsely. "Mr. Harrison wanted me to leave during the party so that there wouldn't be a fuss."

"But it's not *fair*!" I cried. "It's not *right*! I won't let you go, Shannon! Not like this!"

"You did everything you could—more than you had to, much, much more," she replied. "Don't let this ruin your party. Go upstairs, Lady Beth. Go back to the ballroom. Go back and enjoy your special night. Forget all about this."

"I won't," I said stubbornly, blinking back the hot tears that made Shannon's face look blurry. "I won't ever forget, and I won't stop searching for the truth until I've cleared your name."

Then I turned to James. "You *promised* you'd help me," I reminded him. "Please don't take her to the train station! Please!"

"I'm not taking her to the train station," he told me. "At least, not tonight. Shannon will stay at the inn, and I'm to fetch her in the morning for the seven o'clock train. Now, I know what you're going to say, Lady Beth," he continued as I opened my mouth to protest. "But if I don't do as Mr. Harrison says, he'll release me from service."

"Shannon," I begged, "please, please tell me your secret. It's not too late! We can still fix this—you won't have to leave—"

Shannon's eyes glistened in the moonlight. For a moment, she wavered; for a moment, I thought, *Yes, yes, at last, Shannon will tell me everything—*

Then we heard Mrs. Morris's voice. "Tell Mrs. Beaudin that we need more *petits fours*. And *what* is taking them so long in the scullery? We've nearly run out of glasses!"

I could see the same fear on Shannon's and James's faces that I felt in my heart. If I were discovered outside with them instead of inside at my own party, they would both be in terrible trouble.

"Beth, *go!*" Shannon implored me, forgetting my title. "You must sneak back inside. The passage—do you remember—"

"I do," I said in a rush. Then I ran from the car, back into the house, down the corridor, and ducked into the secret passageway that Shannon had showed me before. How dark it was! Without a candle, the cold, damp tunnel was as black as a tomb. This time, I would have to find my way by feel alone.

I yanked off my glove so that I could again use the wall as a guide. The stones were rough against my fingers, and I shivered in my thin silk gown. Faster and faster I walked, stumbling over the uneven floor in my dainty slippers. At last, my fingers grazed against the wooden door frame, and I breathed a sigh of relief at the realization that I had found my way out.

In the library, I held on to the back of a chair to steady myself, exhaling deeply in a long, jagged sigh. Through the window, I saw the motorcar disappear down the drive, carrying Shannon away from Chatswood Manor. In all the commotion, I hadn't even been able to say a proper good-bye to her. A few tears slipped down my cheeks.

"Beth!"

I spun around to find Mother standing in the doorway.

"I've been looking everywhere for you," she continued. "Why did you leave the party? How long have you been here? I searched the library not five minutes ago—oh, my darling, why are you crying?"

"It's all—it's so—"

"There, there, darling; Mummy knows," my mother crooned as she brushed the tears from my cheeks. "It's ever so overwhelming to be the center of attention like this. But you've handled yourself beautifully; in fact, your grandmother and I were just talking about what a brilliant success you'll be at your coming out in a few years.

"Come along now; it's in poor taste to leave your own party, my dear," Mother continued. "I am glad that Gabrielle told me you'd left. The poor girl; all the excitement must've gone to her head, for she told me that you'd gone downstairs to the servants' quarters! Of course, I knew that such a thing could never be true."

Luckily, Mother had spun me around to fluff my curls, so she did not see the look of shock on my face. Had Gabrielle *followed* me? But *why*? And why on earth would she tattle to Mother?

Unless she was trying to keep me from finding out the truth.

"Yes, Mother, we must return at once," I said.

"Of course, dear girl. I'm sure you would hate to miss another moment of your party," she said.

I smiled and nodded, but the truth was, I was desperate for the party to end.

For there was something far more important I needed to do.

13

$\mathcal{T}$he last toast, the last waltz, the last embrace, the last good-bye.

At last, my birthday party was over.

Back in my room, Miss Dalton went quietly about her work, leaving me scrubbed, brushed, changed, and missing Shannon. Before she departed, Miss Dalton left the candle lit at my request; as soon as she was gone, I crawled into bed with Essie Bridges's journal. I had the strangest feeling that there was something in it that would help me solve the mystery of the Trufant locket. I knew that that didn't make much sense; after all, Essie had written those entries long ago. Perhaps I was drawn to the journal because there wasn't anything else I could do to help Shannon. Or perhaps it was wishful thinking. Something told me this journal was my very last chance.

And Shannon's, too.

*Had quite a row with Fannie this morn.
Yesterday I took Sparrow and Lark for a picnic
to take their mind off their mother's illness. We
had a grand time, but by the time we got home,
the girls were frightfully dirty. I whisked off
their pinafores and stuffed them into the laundry
chute, relieved that they would disappear into the
darkness of the basement and reappear in the
twins' wardrobe once they were freshly cleaned.*

*But oh, did I get an earful from Fannie
today. She was none too pleased about the state
of the twins' garments—especially because they
stained all the other clothes when they fell into
the basket below the chute. I have no interest in
making an enemy of the housemaids, so I was
quick to promise Fannie that I would be more
careful in the future about sending filthy clothes
down the laundry chute.*

I sat up in shock; Essie's journal clattered to the floor.

The laundry chute!

How had I missed it before?

135

A cloud of memories from the last few days swirled through my mind:

"Before bed, you must prepare for my Lady Gabrielle fresh strawberries—"

"Jennie took her down a peg. We'll see how fancy she feels after spending every waking moment in the basement!"

"There is an unfortunate stain on your nightgown that will require additional treatment."

"Someone has been throwing garbage *down the laundry chutes!"*

It was a surprising theory—crazy, perhaps—and yet it seemed clear to me that it was the only possibility.

"Oh, Shannon," I whispered in the darkness. "Why didn't you tell me?"

Before dawn, I wrapped my velvet dressing gown around me and snuck through the house. Downstairs, all the lights were shining, and though it was still dark outside, there was a great deal of bustling in the kitchen. I slipped outside, unseen, and leaned against the motorcar. I didn't have long to wait.

James was so startled to see me that he dropped his cap. "Lady Beth!" he exclaimed.

"Shh!" I said with a finger to my lips.

He realized that I was in a dressing gown and immediately averted his eyes. "Please, you've got to go inside," he begged. "It's not proper for you to be out here—"

"I'll go," I told him. "But you must not take Shannon to the train station, James. Bring her here instead."

"You know I can't do that, milady."

"I know that you promised to help me. I'm asking you to keep your promise."

There was a long silence. The sun had begun to rise; the faintest pink streaks glowed on the horizon.

"What do you plan to do?" James finally asked.

"Just bring Shannon to Chatswood," I replied. "Tell her to wait for me in the passage. She'll know what that means."

James sighed deeply. But all he said was, "Lady Beth, I hope you know what you're doing."

So do I, I thought.

I returned to my room and forced myself to stay in bed until Miss Dalton came to dress me, though every inch of me was jittery with apprehension. When it was time for breakfast, I didn't go straight to the dining room. Instead, I made a detour to the library.

I pulled gently on the panel between the book-cases, revealing the gaping blackness of the passage. "Shannon?" I called as loudly as I dared. "Can you hear me?"

She appeared in a few moments, wide-eyed and white as the bed linens. "Oh, Lady Beth, what've you done?" she whispered. "This is wrong, all wrong; I shouldn't be here—"

"Yes, you should," I said firmly as I took her hand. "Shannon, do you trust me?"

There was a pause before she answered. "Yes, Lady Beth. I do."

"Then don't be afraid."

Shannon seemed to be reassured by the confidence in my voice. Thankfully, there was no way for her to know how wildly my heart was pounding. I tried to steady my nerves as I led her to the dining room. It was too late to turn back now.

My head was high as I marched into the dining room with Shannon by my side. Everyone was already at the table: Father and Uncle Claude, Grandmother, Cecily, Gabrielle. The footmen were serving while Mr. Harrison stood against the wall, watching their every move.

All eyes turned to me as a stunned silence filled the room.

Mr. Harrison spoke first. "Shannon Kelley, go downstairs," he ordered in a voice so low that it gave me chills.

Shannon turned to leave, but I held her arm. "No, Mr. Harrison," I said firmly. "She'll stay."

"I say, Beth," Father spoke up. "This is an outrage, really, it is. You'll go to your room at once, and not another word from you."

"No, Father," I said, my voice steady though my hands were trembling. "There is something I must say."

"Harrison, do something about that maid," Father barked. "Beth, I *order* you to go to your room."

I pulled myself up to my full height. "Not until you've heard what I have to say."

"You'll sorely regret your actions today, my girl," Father replied. "Someone fetch her mother."

"Yes," I agreed. "Mother should be here and Aunt Beatrice, too. Oh, and Helena, of course."

The tension in the room was unbearable while we waited for Mother and Aunt Beatrice. Uncle Claude and Grandmother were clearly baffled by my behavior. Cousin Gabrielle succumbed to a nervous fidget, knotting her napkin and drumming her fingers on the table until Uncle Claude told her to stop. Only Cecily seemed to be enjoying herself as she ate scone after scone with a big, toothy grin on her face.

Then Mother and Aunt Beatrice whisked into the dining room in a cloud of ribbons and Parisian perfume. Helena followed them and stood behind Gabrielle's chair.

"Beth, this behavior is so unbecoming," Mother said. "I'm terribly disappointed in you."

"I hope that what I have to say will change your opinion," I told her. Then, with all eyes on me for the second time in twelve hours, I began.

"This is my lady's maid, Shannon Kelley," I said. "You all know that she was accused of stealing the Trufant locket because it was found in a laundry basket in her room. This, despite the fact that Shannon has been a faithful and trustworthy employee at Chatswood for two years."

Uncle Claude threw down his napkin. "Edwin, I thought this matter had been settled," he said to Father.

"Why are we still discussing it?"

"Well, Beth?" Father directed the question to me.

"Because Shannon has been framed, and I'm prepared to prove her innocence!" I announced.

Cousin Gabrielle leaped to her feet. "I will not stay in the same room as a thief!" she cried dramatically.

"Oh, sit down, would you?" Cecily said. "I want to hear what the girl's got to say."

I shot my great-grandmother a grateful smile and continued. "When Gabrielle and I walked in the rose garden, she disparaged the Trufant locket," I began. "She wanted something more valuable, something covered with jewels. Something like the Elizabeth necklace."

"Is this true, Gabrielle?" Uncle Claude said, unable to keep the shock—and sadness—from his voice. "My own mother—your grandmother—wore that locket every day of her life, as did her mother before her, and *her* mother before her. You should be grateful to own jewelry that has belonged to so many great ladies!"

"Papa, it is a terrible lie!" cried Gabrielle—quite unconvincingly.

"I have no reason to lie," I defended myself. "But

please, let me continue. The next day, after I received the Elizabeth necklace, the Trufant locket disappeared. And when Uncle Claude promised Gabrielle a replacement if it wasn't found, she immediately asked for something with lots of jewels.

"But the Trufant locket *was* found," I continued. "In a laundry basket in Shannon's room. I don't think it had been stolen, though. I think it was thrown down a laundry chute and it landed in the basket."

Mother looked confused. "Beth, what is a *laundry chute?*" she asked.

"It's a tunnel in the wall," I explained. "The lady's maids throw our laundry down them so that it arrives in the basement without being carried through the corridors."

"How terribly clever," Mother mused.

"Helena," I said suddenly. She looked up with her lips tightly pursed. "Have you not been throwing Lady Gabrielle's *garbage* in the laundry chutes— those little doors in the walls?"

Helena's eyes darted from side to side. "I did not know!" she exclaimed. "In France we use the chutes for garbage, not the laundry!"

"And did Lady Gabrielle tell you to discard the Trufant locket?" I asked as gently as I could.

"Helena, *shut up!*" Gabrielle shrieked. "Not another word!"

But instead of listening to Gabrielle, Helena burst into tears. "It was an *order*," she sobbed. "What was I to do? I always follow my lady's orders!"

"Gabrielle!" Aunt Beatrice exclaimed. "How *could* you?"

Beside me, I felt Shannon's shoulders relax a bit, but I did not look at her. Not yet.

"So now we know how the locket came to be in the laundry basket," I said. "But that still leaves one more mystery to be solved: Why was Shannon in possession of a laundry basket? After all, that is a task for a housemaid—not a lady's maid."

I turned to Shannon and took her hands in mine. "Shannon, have the housemaids been punishing you for your promotion to lady's maid?" I asked her. "Have they forced you to do the laundry in addition to your other duties?"

"Yes, Lady Beth," Shannon replied, her voice a whisper. Then she cleared her throat and spoke again. "Yes, they have."

"Miss Kelley!" Mr. Harrison spoke up. "I don't need to tell you how unacceptable that is. Mrs. Morris will be outraged to hear it. Why did you stay silent?"

"I didn't want to make it worse," Shannon explained. "And I didn't want them to lose their positions for it."

Mr. Harrison turned to Father. "Lord Etheridge," he said, "given these developments, I find it appropriate to reinstate Miss Kelley immediately—if she'll accept the position of lady's maid once more."

"Oh, would I!" Shannon exclaimed. Then she caught herself and lowered her head. "I would be honored to accept. Thank you, Mr. Harrison."

"You have brought a great shame to the Trufant name, daughter," Uncle Claude said sternly to Gabrielle.

"No, I haven't!" Gabrielle said wildly. She pointed at Helena. "*She* did it! She took my locket and threw it away! It was *her* fault!"

Helena fell to the floor, weeping. "*Non, non, ce n'est pas possible!*" she cried. "I am faithful to my lady; I do whatever she asks of me! I would have never thrown away her locket if she had not asked me to do it!"

"Shannon, please take Helena downstairs so that

she may recover her spirits," Mr. Harrison ordered. "I am sure her employers will discipline her as they see fit."

Shannon obliged at once. But on her way from the dining room, she paused beside me. At the neck of her dress, I could see the coppery glint of her Saint Anthony medal. *The patron saint of lost things and missing people*, I remembered, pleased that every-thing—and everyone—was back in its rightful place.

"Lady Beth," Shannon began. "How can I ever thank you—"

"There's no need, and there never will be," I told her, grinning. "But I'll see you after breakfast, I hope. I'm not satisfied with my hair, though I know Miss Dalton did her best."

Shannon grinned back at me, then hurried Helena from the room. We could hear her sobs echoing down the hallway.

I turned my attention back to my cousin, who looked as though she were on the brink of tears herself. "Gabrielle, why?" I asked. "I was so looking forward to your visit. We've always had such jolly times together. What happened?"

"I would've liked a birthday picnic," she whispered,

staring at the floor. "Or a party. Or a necklace made of precious jewels. My birthday trip to Paris was . . . not as special as I claimed. I thought—I thought it would be easy to celebrate you, Cousin. But it was easier to covet your many fine things. I *am* sorry. I thought the Trufant locket would simply disappear, nothing more."

"You were brought up better than this, Gabrielle," Aunt Beatrice said. "I hope you're aware of how desperately you've embarrassed yourself—and your family. I am canceling our trip to America. You clearly lack the maturity to undertake such a journey."

"*Maman!* No!" Gabrielle exclaimed.

"Enough," Uncle Claude said, holding up his hand. "It has been decided."

"Oh, please, Mother, might I go?" I cried at once. "Oh, *please*? It would mean ever so much to me to be there when Cousin Kate receives the Katherine necklace! I'll be on my very best behavior! I promise!"

Mother and Father looked at each other for a long moment.

"In my day, a girl your age would never go abroad on such a journey," Mother finally said. "But times are changing. And Beth, my dear, you have proven yourself far more capable and resourceful than I ever would have imagined. Perhaps your father and I have under-estimated you, and for that, I am sorry."

I scarcely dared to breathe while I waited for her to continue.

"Yes," she said at last. "Yes, I think it's high time you met the other half of the Chatswood dynasty . . . with Shannon to accompany you, of course."

"Thank you, Mother; thank you, Father!" I cried as I rushed to embrace them. "This is the most excit-ing day of my life! I promise I will be perfectly well behaved—a credit to the Chatswood line!"

A loud laugh filled the room as Cecily rose from the table. "Well, you've already done better by the Etheridge line than that shifty cousin of yours, my girl," she announced. "You've got pluck—just like your great-grandmother Katherine. I daresay she'd be proud of you."

"Great-Grandmother *Elizabeth*," I corrected Cecily. I knew it was rude, but I couldn't help myself.

Father and Aunt Beatrice exchanged an uncom-fortable glance, troubled by Cecily's wandering mind. "Come along now, Grandmother," Aunt Beatrice said.

"I think you need some rest."

Then she turned to Gabrielle. "And you'll take the rest of your meals in your room today, young lady," she said. "I hope that will be ample time for all the apologies you need to compose."

"Beth, please sit and eat something," Mother instructed me. "I think we've all had enough excitement for one morning."

I immediately slid into my chair as Mr. Harrison stepped forward to pour my tea. I was so excited that I couldn't possibly imagine eating a single bite. But I would, of course. Mother and Father expected me to behave like an adult, and I had every intention of meeting their expectations. But that didn't mean I had to stop daydreaming about what was to come. A smile spread across my face as my fingers rested upon the Elizabeth necklace around my neck.

To travel all the way to America . . . to see the Katherine necklace with my own two eyes . . . to celebrate Cousin Kate's birthday with her . . . to meet Kate *and* my Great-Great-Aunt Katherine at last . . . and to finally, *finally* find the answers to some of my questions . . .

The excitement of my summer had scarcely begun!

Beth's story is far from over . . .

Find out what happens when she journeys to America to meet her cousin Kate in

Kate's Story, 1914

" 'Then, with quaking hand, her ladyship reached for the rusty key hanging on the wall—' "

"Kate."

My mother's voice wafted to us from the doorway. I dropped my book as my lady's maid, Nellie, leaped to her feet. *Rats*, I thought. If it wasn't bad enough that Nellie and I had been caught reading when I should've been getting ready, now I'd lost my place in *The Hidden History of Castle Claremont*. And just when we were *finally* about to learn Lady Marian's secret!

"I trust you're ready for the meeting," Mother said with a pointed look at my stocking feet.

"Yes, Mother," I said as Nellie and I reached for my shoes at the same time, cracking our heads together. "Ow! I mean, I'm nearly ready. Just look at my hair.

Didn't Nellie work wonders with it?"

"Very stylish," Mother said as a smile flickered across her lips. She always tried to be stern when she caught me breaking the rules, but she could never completely stop her smiles.

Nellie curtsied quickly. "Thank you, ma'am. Will there be anything else?"

"No, Nellie. I'll escort Kate to the garden myself," Mother replied.

With another curtsy and a nod of her head, Nellie scurried from the room.

Mother fixed her eyes on me. "Kate," she repeated.

"I know. And I'm sorry. I was ready, really I was. I just had to put my shoes on!" My words tumbled out in a rush. "See, it's my fault—not Nellie's. She loves to read but never has time, so when she does my hair, I read aloud so we can both enjoy the story. So you see, she really didn't do anything wrong—"

"No one is blaming Nellie."

I stopped talking. Mother slipped her arm through mine as we walked into the hallway.

"Kate, sweetheart, you're almost twelve years old," Mother continued. "It's high time you started acting like a Vandermeer in all that you say and do."

"But I—"

"I appreciate Nellie's love of stories. And she is welcome to spend her day off curled up with a book. But you must set an example for her. After all, if you don't behave as you're supposed to, how will Nellie and the other servants understand what is expected of them?"

We had almost reached the door. Mother paused and held both my hands. "You're ready, Kate," she said. "That's why your great-grandmother and I have decided that you've earned the privilege of attending your first meeting of the Bridgeport Beautification Society today. Sooner than you think, you'll be taking your place in society beside us. I'm sure I don't have to remind you how important the next eight days are."

I grinned at Mother. As if I could forget! In just over a week, my twelfth birthday would arrive at last. I would finally receive the Katherine necklace, a precious family heirloom that had been passed down to every Katherine in my family since my great-grandmother had received it on her twelfth birthday many years ago. Her twin sister, Elizabeth, had received a necklace, too. Each one was shaped like half a golden heart, but that was where the similarities ended. Elizabeth's necklace was set with shimmering blue sapphires, while Katherine's glittered with red rubies—the twins' favorite colors. The necklaces were as meaningful as they were beautiful, for they were the last gift that the twins' mother, Lady Mary Chatswood, my great-great-grandmother, had selected for the girls before she died.

I'd heard the stories for years: that Elizabeth and Katherine were inseparable from the moment they were born. And they looked so much alike that their mother was the only one who could truly tell them apart. But only one twin could marry the heir to their English estate and become the next lady of Chatswood Manor. After Elizabeth became engaged to Cousin Maxwell, Great-Grandmother Katherine married my great-grandfather Alfred Vandermeer, and he brought her back to his home in America. Not soon after, my great-grandfather founded Vandermeer Steel, and the Vandermeer fortune grew and grew, what with Vandermeer Steel incorporated in nearly every building, bridge, and train track constructed from then until this very day. His success enabled him to make his family home on the cliffs overlooking the ocean even grander. Today, Vandermeer Manor has seventy-five rooms, four separate wings, five floors, and eight gardens. For many people in our town, it is the largest building they've ever seen. But for me, it is home. And though Lady Elizabeth Chatswood never set foot in Vandermeer Manor, her great-granddaughter, Beth—my cousin—would arrive here in just five days! I was so excited to meet Beth at last that I could hardly think about anything else. We knew each other only through letters, but it was obvious that we had so much in common. Our birthdays were just one month apart, and as the first girls in our generation, we shared the privilege of being named after the original Elizabeth and Katherine. I love my Great-Grandmother Katherine more than words can say, and I am honored to be her namesake. And I knew that Beth felt the same way about her name, even though her great-grandmother Elizabeth had died before Beth was born.

"Make me proud today, Kate," Mother said to me as Emil, one of the footmen, stepped forward to open the doors to the garden. "Like you always do."

Instantly, I put on my best, brightest smile. It had seemed so vain to practice it in the mirror, but now I was glad that Mother had insisted. "When all eyes are on you, you'll find it hard to smile naturally," she had told me. And she was right.

CAN'T STOP
THINKING ABOUT THE

SECRETS
of the MANOR?

Find a family tree, character histories, excerpts,
and more at **SecretsoftheManor.com**